INSIDE AWAKE

By
Romé Sims

Eloquent Books
New York, New York

Copyright © 2009
All rights reserved — Romé Sims

No part of this book may be reproduced or transmitted in any form or by any means, graphic, electronic, or mechanical, including photocopying, recording, taping, or by any information storage retrieval system, without the permission, in writing, from the publisher.

Eloquent Books
An imprint of AEG Publishing Group
845 Third Avenue, 6th Floor – 6016
New York, NY 10022
www.eloquentbooks.com

ISBN: 978-1-60693-912-3   1-60693-912-2

Printed in the United States of America

Book Design: D. Johnson, Dedicated Business Solutions, Inc.

Thank U's

To Melody and Olivia
No words will ever exist that can truly express my love for you both.

To Leanne
In the mist of despair and darkness, you gave comfort. You have been blessed with the rarest of wisdoms. Yours is a special soul.

To John
Your brotherly love and understanding kept me growing.

To Mary
Your kindness and devotion will not go unanswered.

To him that is He
Everyone is running from something. But if we're lucky, very lucky, he intervenes and presents an opportunity to conquer our fears. Only then, if triumphant, can a destiny he has bestowed become a destiny fulfilled.

INSIDE AWAKE

Chapter One
Lake Eyasi, Tanzania

The terrain is deep rusted-red. Abundant dirt and dust permeate trees, shrubs, and the local wildlife. After an hour of uncomfortable driving southwest of Serengeti National Park and the Ngorongoro Crater, a small team of scientists from the Tanzania Wildlife Research Institute had arrived at the northern shore of Lake Eyasi.

"Did anyone else see something weird a few miles back?" asked one of the men.

"Weird? Weird like how?"

"A light. I saw a strange bright light."

"Did you walk toward it?" a female associate asked, smiling.

"Never ever walk into the light," said another.

"No no, not that kind of light," said the scientist. "This thing was hovering or maybe floating just above some trees."

"Hovering or floating huh? You're not getting out of this assignment that easy," said the team leader with a grin.

The trip was unscheduled. Fearing an avian flu outbreak, the agency sent personnel across the country once a year to trap and collect random blood samples from migratory birds that used the waters of Tanzania as temporary sanctuaries. Researchers had assessed the region several months earlier, with the resulting field tests showing no bird flu viruses present. Later, unconfirmed reports of dead waterfowl found floating in the lake demanded a more thorough investigation.

The team removed a canoe from the roof of one of the vehicles and carried it to the lake. A brightly colored lizard ran toward the underbrush, startled by the intrusion. High atop an acacia tree, a goshawk stared down from its perch. The bird tilted its head left, then right, and then left again, as if perplexed by the unusual activity.

Masaii tribes moved into the Ngorongoro and the Serengeti over a century ago, pushing the Datoga and other, weaker indigenous Bushmen living there to the south. Many made Lake Eyasi and the surrounding savanna their home. Their water-filled footprints were abundant in the soft mud. Green and yellow butterflies drank from the imprints.

Located on the floor of the Great Rift Valley and dominated by the Crater Highlands to the north, the lake was slightly alkaline and stretched fifty-one kilometers to the south. Collecting blood samples would take a number of days due to the vastness of the area. Two researchers paddled the canoe toward the middle of Lake Eyasi while the rest of the team set up tents and bird traps on shore.

Along a sandy embankment on the opposite shoreline, a troop of baboons nervously quenched their thirst. Highly intelligent and with well-developed social skills, several sentinels watched closely as hungry crocodiles slowly patrolled the shallows. Neither graceful nor beautiful, a warthog and her young paced nervously back and forth along a rocky patch of the shoreline; she grunted, observing the baboons, awaiting a signal that it was safe to drink. Hippopotami cooled themselves from the unrelenting and overbearing heat. A mother and her calf playfully chased a Marabou stork; it squawked irritably, then flew away, discarding a few soft white feathers. The calf gazed skyward with mouth agape, taunting the retreating fowl.

Further south, adult elephants partially submerged themselves while the youthful frolicked in the cool waters around them. Unable to resist, the herd's matriarch joined in. She grasped a small leafy branch with her trunk and playfully chased them. Weary of the game, her daughter's offspring turned to face her pursuer. She lifted her trunk and sounded a defiant bellow. The calf's boldness briefly startled the elephant. She blew a louder trumpet of her own as the chase resumed.

Children playing in the shallows to escape escalating temperatures watched as, in the deepest waters of the lake, an invisible force stirred the surface from beneath. The area churned and steamed with an intensifying radiance. An orb surrounded by a cloud of blue mist slowly lifted skyward. The disturbance frightened a large flock of sparrows and long-tailed starlings. Screeching loudly, they flew en masse further south.

The mysterious orb hovered silently, then split into four parts, then eight, and then finally back to one. Frightened, the children raced to alert their families of the unsettling magic.

#

The chief of the clan, Mamoya, sat with the men beneath a Balanites tree. He recounted tales of birds so abundant they blocked out the sun, and herds of animals so large they shook the earth. With sparkling eyes, Mamoya held his bow tightly as he recalled his younger years.

His wife sat with the women that nursed small babies. Whispering to the other wives, she smiled broadly at her husband. They giggled as the men took turns narrating suspect hunting tales.

The nomadic Datoga settled temporarily wherever they found food and water. Because animals tended to avoid humans, the nomadic people roamed far away from populated areas. In groups of four or five families, they built no houses or structures. Instead, they lived in the shade of trees, using animal skins as beds and seats. The women gathered fruit, tubers and water while the men hunted birds and wild animals with bows and arrows. Although their scant attire included various pieces picked up from westerners, they wore mostly hides.

In the midst of the Datoga dwellings, marked by upright sticks in semi-circles, baboon carcasses cooked slowly on long sticks over small fires. Aromas of decaying flesh and fruit enticed flies and other insects. Nearby, a leopard sought refuge from the heat in the shade of an acacia tree. She twitched her tail occasionally, entertaining her cubs. Vervet monkeys attempted to evict the unwelcome felines by dropping twigs and leaves from overhead. The leopard glared at the primates, displaying her teeth as they chattered excessively. Under constant bombardment, she departed in search of less inhospitable shelter for herself and her young.

Keyabu, the bravest and strongest of the children, was the first to arrive at the temporary campsite.

"Mother, father! Aseeta the Creator has called the water spirits home," he said, breathing heavily. "He woke them from the abyss with wind from the nostrils of the buffalo. They gathered in the heavens to watch the hippopotamus, the crocodile and the fish. Then the water spirits grew angry and forced the animals to flee from their sacred places."

Other children arrived a few moments later and gave their accounts of the eerie incident. Some suspected the children of concocting a ruse, while the elders of the clan were less skeptical. After several minutes of heated debate, Mamoya dispatched a small group of hunters to investigate.

#

The frightened men stood on the bank of Lake Eyasi staring in awe at a white pulsating radiance. It hovered silently just above the surface. The object rotated rapidly on its axis, sending a violent wind through Acacia and Baobab trees, releasing their fruit. A low-pitched hum resonated across the savannah as its appearance changed to a silvery metallic. Dimmer blue and red orbs suddenly burst forth, radiating waves of an invisible force. The orbs raced skyward followed by a smaller white glow and then vanished. Badly burned from the radiance's intensity, the hunters, animals, and most members of the Tanzania Wildlife Research Institute, perished where they stood.

#

Several days passed before the Tanzanian government called in the United Nations to assist in investigating the strange phenomenon. The Helos and Huey helicopters with familiar white UN lettering landed on the east side of the lake, their rotors kicking up red dirt and dust. Doctor Kikwete, the head of field operations for the Tanzanian Ministry of Health, prepared to explain to the group as succinctly as possible what had happened, and why his government had contacted the UN to look into the incident that occurred four days ago. The "thing" that had erupted from Lake Eyasi, according to statements made by a survivor before he died, was the source of the death and destruction. The doctor considered the account unexplainable and incomprehensible to him, and his colleagues. He met the leader of the health investigators with barely controlled fury as scientists dressed in full biohazard suits disembarked.

"What the hell is this? I told the director that there was no evidence of Ebola or any other viral contamination," he yelled over the aircraft engines.

"We prefer to run our own test, Dr. Kikwete," said Doctor Alba, the head field coordinator as the whirling rotors subsided. "It's protocol."

Her team split up, examining the surroundings. Some held toxic and infectious agent detectors while a few carried Geiger counters and other portable scientific devices.

"I'm Dr. Leanne Alba and this is Doctors Bob Walsh, Claude Levitte, and Winnie Kagame. If you'll kindly take us to your medical tents, we'd like to take a look at the bodies. Claude, take the Mortuary Operational Response Team and make sure all universal blood-borne pathogen protocols are being followed."

Two members of her team who had been taking water and air samples at the lake, ran toward them.

"We've got something," said one.

"Bag it and tag it," said Dr. Alba. "And get those samples off to the Uganda lab ASAP."

She turned her attention back to Dr. Kikwete.

"After you, sir."

A Tanzanian national task force had set up a small field hospital unit to identify and contain the potential biological threat. Nearly filled to capacity, a number of portable morgue tents were adjacent to the temporary camp.

Escorted by Dr. Kikwete, Drs. Alba, Walsh and Kagame entered the main medical tent. Three burnt corpses lay on steel tables, each recently autopsied.

"A few of the bodies were examined in here," he said. "After ruling out viral or bacterial agents, a study of the bone fractures and the position of the remains indicated they died from extreme thermal shock."

"It must have been instantaneous. These three don't show any evidence of voluntary self-protective reactions or agony contortions," said Dr. Kagame. "They were killed before they had time to display a reaction—probably in less than a fraction of a second."

Dr. Alba walked around the examining tables, peering in the mouth of each victim with a small flashlight.

"Bob, go over the autopsy reports with Dr. Kikwete. See if they missed anything."

She removed the breathing apparatus from her face and nodded to her colleagues.

"I don't know what it is, but it's definitely not chemical or biological. Winnie, you and I will do a few independent examinations just to see if we can narrow it down."

At the lake's shore, a field scientist collected a water sample. She removed a small plastic bag from her pocket and poured the substance into the test tube. The mixture fizzled, then glowed slightly. She emptied the contents back into the lake, removed a leaf from a nearby shrub and repeated the process. The scientist moved down the shore a few hundred yards. Barely recognizable in the dark wet mud, the burnt remains of a frog rested peacefully next to a fallen acacia tree. After kneeling, she removed forceps from a kit attached to her belt and then collected samples of the amphibian's ashes into a square glass tube. She opened a pouch on the leg of the biohazard suit and pulled out a small black device. After inserting the tube into it, green and red lights rotated around its surface. The analysis complete, the scientist placed a call on her satellite phone.

#

On spacious grounds on the east side of Midtown Manhattan, on the twenty-eighth floor of a golden rectangular building, two men sat in an office. The owner of the office stared out the dark glass windows at the East River below. A double-decker tour boat slowly cruised by.

"Look at them—living out their little insignificant lives without a worry in the world except rent, car and cable TV payments. A life with such trivial concerns—do you remember having such a luxury?"

The other man sat in a leather chair smoking a large cigar. He leaned forward and flicked ashes into a wastebasket next to the desk.

"Nope, can't say I've ever had the pleasure," he replied.

"Knowledge wields a double-edged sword Mister Smith. Unbeknownst to most people on this planet, the world is more dangerous than ever and it's up to people like you and me to make sure they never find that out so that they may go on collecting their acorns, or preparing their dens without worry. Without any knowledge of the true lies they live."

"Speaking of which, have you heard anything from Tanzania?" asked Mister Smith.

"Patience, Mister Smith, patience."

The man looked at his watch.

"I'm expecting a call any moment now."

The phone on the desk rang.

"This is Mister Westmore speaking."

"This is Jones at the Tanzania site. Test results from Lake Eyasi indicate positive, sir."

"Are you sure?"

"I have confirmation from water, animal and plant tissue samples."

"Good work, Jones. I want you to contact Colonel Schomberg of the Security Council's Military Staff Committee and pack your bags for Antarctica."

He hung up the phone and looked out the window.

"Mister Smith, notify the Security Council president we have on-site verification from Tanzania."

Chapter Two
European Laboratory for Particle Physics Complex, Switzerland, Building LL7

"Powering rare isotope accelerator and initializing spectral analysis sequencer. Thirteen percent beryllium, two percent niobium, eighty-five percent unknown," said the lab technician.

Perplexed, Doctor David Woodall stared at the mysterious artifact. A wave of uncertainty washed over him like an early morning tide.

"What went wrong? Were the calculations too far off? Maybe this is impossible," soundless voices breathed in his ear.

The whispers of his demons had haunted him practically all his life. *Dreams were just that, dreams: unattainable and unrealistic. Fantasies created to escape an inescapable monotonous and dreadful life.* In any endeavor, the malevolent forces tormented him relentlessly until self-doubt strangled any meaningful undertaking.

Part of a large family of twelve, he'd grown up in the urban slums of Atlanta, Georgia. Urban blight was detrimental to the social and economic well being of the community, and it affected him and his family immensely. Conditions rarely afforded an opportunity for new clothing or shoes. It embarrassed him to wear old ones with holes to school or a shirt worn the previous day by his brother. A scarcity of necessities contributed incalculably to his lack of confidence . . . a confidence he would spend years fighting to regain.

Pulling a CD from a slot above his monitor, David slid across the room on his chair and loaded it into another computer drive. He checked and compared his backup data.

"Hmmmm," he mumbled to himself. "No errors here."

He slid across the room again to the main terminal under the observation chamber.

"How's it going, David old boy? Did you mustah any favorable results from the spectral analysis?" asked a voice from the intercom near the door. David recognized the voice instantly.

Cambridge educated William Jamison was a world-renowned physicist with advanced degrees in bio-genetics, astrophysics and a long list of others. He was also a pompous, egocentric, insufferable British snob. A descendent of aristocratic bloodlines, he spoke the stereotypical dialect of nobility and royalty. It conveyed the impression that not only was he better than most people, but he was also keenly aware of the fact.

Several years ago, while researching dark energy, he was involved in an unauthorized experiment that tragically killed several workers at the Institute for Nuclear Research in Frankfurt. Although a maverick, Doctor Jamison was nevertheless a brilliant scientist.

David typed several keystrokes into the main terminal.

"I'm still having problems getting it stabilized," he replied.

"I'm terribly sorry, but tell me, Dr. Woodall, do you comprehend the time restraints we are undah here? Leave the results on my desk so one can take a butchah at them."

David continued to enter his data.

"By the way, we won't be meeting this afternoon. Jill'll be commuting to Berlin to a meeting tomorrow so I'll have to jolly well go over the blooming numbers with her before she departs. So stop gaddin' about and fetch me your backup files."

Ignoring him, David stared at his computer model.

"Woodall!" snapped Doctor Jamison through the intercom.

Only a nod and a soft "got it" came as a reply.

"One thinks dah bloke's bloody off his trolley. Let myself know if there are any improvements," Dr. Jamison whispered to one of the technicians.

He turned his attention back to David.

"Give me a ring up when you're finished and have the relic sent to the technicians on B level. They can leg it; more multi-spectral imagin' testing on it—and Woodall—take a couple of days so you can mustah a fresh start."

Frustrated by David's lack of progress, Dr. Jamison left the observation deck.

He'd opposed Dr. Woodall's appointment and argued vigorously against it. They had met in college becoming, to a certain extent, rivals. While David was judicious and pragmatic, Doctor Jamison was a risk taker. To him, ethical implications of scientific discovery were unimportant. Only "pure science" unobstructed by a misguided sense of morality could solve the mysteries of the universe. Dr. Woodall had seen his impudent attitude before. To David, the lack of compassion, empathy and principles were all indications of a restless self-serving soul, qualities he sometimes associated with his father—a father he never knew.

A heavy drinker on the weekends and moneyless during the week, Thomas Woodall made life a living hell for everyone. He was quiet and seemingly an indifferent man. Once in awhile David could coax a smile from him. He loved baseball and occasionally they'd watch games together on TV. David never understood what made his father happy or sad, but they were probably as close as his father would ever be to anyone.

David discovered many things about himself during years of self-reflection and research. Depression, anxiety, and low self-esteem were typical of a child of an alcoholic parent. Feelings of rejection and the constant fear of emotional loss is a common personality characteristic. Through self-reflection came the realization that he was still that frightened child from so long ago. He was still that child that witnessed, his father hitting his mother, the child that dreaded the weekends because of his fathers heavy drinking. The child that lay awake at night afraid to sleep, hoping nothing dreadful would happen. Living in fear took a heavy toll on David, but he finally forgave his father. Looking back at it now, his dad must have been under considerable pressure to withdraw the way he did. David never understood the conditions or the defining moment that drove his destructive behavior, or which domino triggered the unstoppable events that led to his downward spiral. However, he was determined not to let life's circumstances lead him down that same path. Yes, he was haunted by his past. Sometimes the past is difficult to escape, and sometimes the past won't let you escape.

#

Didier, a French graduate student, approached Doctor Jamison in the corridor.

"Docteur Willoughby veut vous voir dans la salle de commande d'accélérateur de partilcle."

Annoyed, Doctor Jamison shook his head. The student held up a forefinger and removed a small, red white and blue book from his lab coat. Awkwardly flipping through the pages, he tried in English.

"Ahhhh—telephone, no, no. *Aucune attente de non*. Wait," he said nervously.

"Blimey! The bloke's a bloody bucket," thought Jamison.

He had no patience for students and disliked the non-English speaking ones most of all. Not that he didn't speak French; he spoke five different languages. Since he was an Englishman, he expected everyone to speak English to him. The student tried again.

"Mister Willoughby . . ."

"You mean, Doctor Willoughby?" Doctor Jamison asked irritably.

"Yes, yes, Dr. Willoughby."

"Well fancy that. What about Dr. Willoughby?"

Didier's hands trebled as he fumbled through more pages. He looked up, noticing Dr. Jamison's sunken brow. Didier pointed down the corridor.

"Doctor Willoughby, for you," he said nervously.

"Ahhhh the smashing French," mumbled Doctor Jamison in his English accent.

He nodded his head in acknowledgment.

"Okay, okay," he said loudly.

He then headed toward the particle accelerator.

In the lab, Dr. Woodall ended his analysis and headed for the Hotel de la Paix where all scientists stayed while working at the Switzerland complex.

Chapter Three
Indian Ocean Sunda Trench Deep Oceanographic Surveyor Expedition

The research vessel USS Argo passed across the Malacca Strait at midnight, then arrived at the survey area off the Sumatra Island at 06:30.

The mythical Argo was the ship built by Argos with the help of Athena, in which Jason and the Argonauts sailed in quest of the Golden Fleece. Its crew included Heracles, Orpheus, and a host of other heroes from all over Greece. Athena fitted the bow of the ship with a speaking timber, cut from the sacred oaks of Dodona. This Argo was also an extraordinary ship and had an exceptional crew.

It had taken eleven years to build her and they spared no expense, nor excluded any innovative technology when it came to equipping her during construction. Most of the hardware and software was highly classified, which created rumors of alien technology onboard. Under extreme conditions, the Mars reconnaissance Orbiter and Rovers performed magnificently and lasted years beyond their life expectancy. NASA's Advance Concept Division designed both, and reports of a new and radical craft in development persisted in the media. Multiple Radar Systems slated for the next "after the next generation of space" telescopes, a newly developed Hydro Ion Propulsion System, and much, much more . . . all part of the largest Black Projects Program ever.

Only a year old and straight out of what the Intel community jokingly called the Mon Calamari Shipyards, the Argo was on her maiden voyage with her submersibles, the Pegasus and the optimum armament arrayed Cerberus.

A warm breeze seduced the vessel as she sat soaking up the morning sun. Whispering clouds peered down between firmaments of azure, while wavelets ridden by white horses caressed her bow. Evicted from a breakfast of mackerel, a vociferous pelican voiced its contempt as it flew off into the distance.

On the northern part of the Ache Basin, in the western part of the research area, the submersible Pegasus launched. After stopping in Sumatra to replenish supplies, Doctor Sharon Geraldos' team had arrived aboard the USS Argo just days earlier. Geri, a nickname given to her by her father, peered through a side portal as the submersible approached the wall of an undersea landslide. An earlier expedition calculated the event transpired roughly eighteen thousand years ago during an underwater earthquake.

At first glance, the dark, cold, remote ocean floor seemed vast, a desolate area of mud and silt. Lieutenant-Commander Tarkenston switched the imaging and lighting systems from one end of the electromagnetic spectrum to the other, revealing a deep sea of the bizarre and an extraordinary mix of bioluminescent creatures. Some were as black as night with light organs on strategic places used to lure unexpected animals to prey on. Others with no pigment at all, had large eyes to gather as much light as possible. A three-foot gulper eel with a hinged skull hung motionless, awaiting its next victim. Its incredibly large mouth opened and closed slowly, tasting the current for any nearby and unsuspecting victims. Transparent viperfish slowly swam by the forward hemispherical dome, staring at the submersible's occupants with big bulging glowing eyes. Its long dorsal fin of photophores attracted crustaceans and small fish near long fang-like teeth. A 15-foot shark gently rammed the submersible before turning and swimming slowly into the darkness.

"Wow, that was a Greenland shark," said Geri. "Maybe they come here to mate. Turn off the lights, Mr. Tarkenston. Let's see what we're really missing."

The cold darkness revealed her secrets as abyssal copepods danced an illuminant waltz.

A voice boomed into her earpiece, startling Dr. Geraldo.

"How's it going, Geri? Any noise on the radar yet?"

She turned down the volume.

"Just the fins and faces of some unfamiliar deep ocean friends so far . . . it's beautiful," replied Geri from over three miles down.

A deep-sea octopus slowly drifted into view. It flapped its tentacles leisurely, pirouetting as it retreated into the depths.

"You might want to tell the pilot to throttle back on the rpm's. I wouldn't want to have to dig you out."

"Don't worry. I doubt if the Navy would let us borrow another billion dollar piece of machinery if we lost this one."

Pegasus came to rest several more miles down, on a ledge adjacent to huge pillars. They seemed out of place in the surrounding underwater topography. Geri assumed the structures, covered with a foot or more of silt, had probably been exposed due to recent seismic activity in the area.

#

"Which scanning package is deployed on the Pegasus Mack?" Captain Bonar asked a radar operator.

"She's operating with a full array, sir."

"Mike," Geri radioed to the surface. "I think I've got something down here".

A revolutionary design allowed the craft to hover in the water column silently, creating no turbulence or heat signature for the curious to observe.

"There's an abnormality . . . the . . ."

Almost indistinguishable from one another, the words leapt from her mouth.

"There's a statue! A statue," she whispered to herself.

Several large lights from the submersible illuminated an enormous partially covered stone figure.

"Come again, Geri? I didn't read your last transmission. You'd better get topside. You've been down three hours and the captain wants the vehicle checked out before tomorrow's dive."

Geri continued staring out the forward hemispherical dome.

"Okay, we're on the way."

After recalibrating the Pegasus, Lieutenant-Commander Tarkenston started the submersible toward the surface. At 2,953 feet, he throttled back on the thrusters.

"Pegasus to Argo, Pegasus to Argo."

"Go ahead, LC."

"Sir, I've got multiple contacts on radar—058 degrees off the port bow."

"Switch to infrared and hold your position," radioed Captain Bonar.

"Mike, you got anything?" he asked a radar operator.

"Maybe—I got something on acoustics—not enough though. Tell him to amplify the subs hydrophone array and patch it through to the AI."

"LC, increase the power to the transducers and send the sound topside."

"Aye, aye, sir."

"Mike?"

"Sperm whales, sir—the AI identified them as sperm whales—three of them."

"Good job, Mike. LC, you got three whales off your port. You are clear to proceed."

"Whales? They must be sperm whales this deep. Let's take a closer look," said Geri.

"I don't know, ma'am. We've been ordered back to the ship."

"Come on, Mr. Tarkenston . . . just for a couple of minutes."

"Pegasus to Argo."

"Go ahead, LC," responded the captain.

"Pegasus requesting delay to observe unusual deep sea life-forms."

"Tell Geri fifteen minutes. No more," said Captain Bonar.

Chapter Four
Polanco, Uruguay

At a site twelve kilometers outside of Polanco, paleontologists painstakingly brushed surrounding matrix from the remarkably preserved skeletal remains of a forty-foot carnivorous beast. An oil and gas exploration team stumbled upon the fossil after a flash flood originating from a nearby semi-plateau.

"*Debemos salir de la tierra sagrada*," said one of the local workers.

"What did he say?" Doctor Edwin Doyle, the leading authority on the dig, asked.

Thousands of mosquitoes and biting flies hovered about, constantly interrupting the excavation. All attempts to fight them off were ineffective.

"He say we must cover the bones and leave the sacred ground," a worker from the local area replied in broken English.

"*Parar cavar. Los antepasados castigarán a los que deshonren este lugar*," said another.

He pointed toward the sky where a lone King Vulture circled silently overhead.

Britney Halliburton, one of Doctor Doyle's brightest and most gifted undergraduate students spoke up.

"They want us to stop digging and something about espirituosas angry."

Frustrated, Doctor Doyle demanded the man leave immediately.

"Espirituosas?" one of the German members of the team asked another.

"It means spirit or spirits," said Britney. "Legend has it a race of people called the Charrúa once inhabited this area. Other tribes were afraid of them because they had hideous, disfigured forms. They thought the Gods had cursed them."

"*Ich hasse in Südamerika arbeiten,*" replied the other German student.

"My God, not the Germans, too," Dr. Doyle muttered.

Removing his hat, he wiped the sweat from his brow with a red bandana. He slapped the back of his neck, crushing a malevolent black fly between his fingers.

"The Charrúa occupied this area during the lithic era," he added.

Other team members gathered around him.

Employed by the Chicago Museum of Natural History and the University of Illinois, Dr. Edwin Doyle was a leading expert in his field and had named over one thousand species of fossilized animals. A mixture of Indiana Jones and Jack Sparrow, captain of the Black Pearl, he wore a brown, Stetson Elk River hat with matching plaid shirt and Ride Packer boots. The renowned paleontologist was the most popular of all the staff at the university, and students waited in long lines just to attend his lectures.

"In the sequence of North and South America prehistoric cultural stages, the lithic stage was the earliest period of human occupation in the Americas, covering the earliest Pleistocene period. Now—ladies and gentlemen, I can go on and on and give you an in-depth history and study of archaeology or anthropology, but today—today, we're paleontologists. I suggest everybody get back to work and forget about local folklore and mythology."

Waving his bandana, he tried dispersing hungry mosquitos whirling about his head.

"Britney, you're in charge. I'll be in my quarters."

Polanco was in the southern subtropical zone of the South American Continent, which meant comfortable warm summers and mild winters. During the summer months, the average temperature ranged from seventy to eighty degrees, although it could occasionally rise into the nineties. The predominantly flat landscape was vulnerable to rapid changes as weather fronts swept across the plains. The area consisted of rolling grass-covered plains, broken by broad-wooded valleys and slow-moving rivers. Low hills sprinkled with huge granite rocks dotted the horizon.

"Doctor Dr., we've found something," a student from the field study course yelled.

The paleontologist hurried out of his tent just in time to see the student lifting a grey, octagonal, prism-shaped box. He handed Dr. Doyle the strange artifact.

"Where did you find this?" he asked.

"Here, near the skull," the student pointed.

"This can't be right. It's nearly in pristine condition and I'm sure the bones are at least one hundred ninety-five million years old," said Dr. Doyle.

Britney touched the object's surface.

"Maybe someone placed it here recently," she said.

"That's highly unlikely. Besides, there's no evidence the site's been previously disturbed."

Doctor Dr. knelt down and brushed away dirt from the teeth of the fossil's massive jaws.

"I want you, and you and you," he said pointing to each, "to delicately remove the surrounding matrix around the tail then hopefully, we can ship it out of here by next Thursday. The rest of you work around the skull and body. Remember the process of fossil preparation is a long and tedious one. Every fossil is different and so is the surrounding matrix. Some techniques may not be useful. With a little luck, in about eight weeks we'll have the entire specimen back at the Center. In the meantime, I'm going to take this and make a few phone calls."

He slowly walked back toward his tent, turning the relic left to right then right to left, unable to find an opening. After rubbing more dirt away, he noticed bizarre symbols. Fascinated, Dr. Doyle held it up to the sun. Hidden symbols appeared. He entered his tent and immediately searched his bag for his satellite phone.

After removing the battery and replacing it with a spare charging by the generator, the scientist placed a call to Chicago.

"Hello? Hello, Hello, Henry? Damn satellite phones. Henry, are you there. Henry, can you hear me?" he asked loudly. "I've found something . . . something extraordinary—at a site outside of Polanco. No, no. Polanco-Polanco, Uruguay. It's a grey octagonal-shaped box with symbols on it. Huh—symbols but no numbers. It has . . . they're similar to hieroglyphs. No, I said hieroglyphs."

The call became inaudible.

"Henry, I'm getting a lot of static."

He placed the object on his cot and hit the phone against his other hand several times.

"Damn phone," he muttered.

"I'll send this to you at the museum tomorrow. See if you can figure out what the symbols mean. Yes, be back in about two months. Hello—hello, hello . . . Oh crap!"

After an abrupt burst of static, the phone disconnected. Dr. Doyle sat on his bunk tinkering with the object late into the night.

The next morning he awoke, the artifact resting on his chest. He grabbed a magnifying glass and sat up on his cot. While re-examining it, Dr. Doyle noticed subtle changes on its surface that were absent the night before. He called for his assistant.

"Britney . . . Britney Halliburton," he shouted.

"Yes sir."

Hoping to locate other fossils, she had been working the far side of a stream searching for clues.

"I'm going to Chicago for about a week. You'll be in charge. Think you can handle it?"

"You can count on me, Dr. Doyle," she responded eagerly.

"Good, tell Alvarez to get a truck ready to take me to Polanco."

Chapter Five
Antarctica
66° 33' 39" S
Polheim Station

"We'd better get back to camp," the scientist yelled over the howling wind. "I'm not sure this is going to let up anytime soon. Matter of fact, I think it's getting worse."

Kyle Lentz, from the US Geological Survey, dismounted his snowmobile and removed a GPS from his Chinook coat pocket.

"We're almost at the coordinates," he replied, pointing to a barely recognizable nearby ridge. "Bout' another half a mile."

He brushed frozen snow from his mustache and beard.

"We'll set up the equipment there and get the hell back to camp."

Struggling through the snowstorm with the lead snowmobile pulling a large sled, they rode on. Without warning, it ran into an unusually sharp depression. The vehicle bounced twice up a jagged incline causing the driver to temporarily lose control. Moments later, it came to a circuitous and unexpected halt. Looking down around his feet, Doctor Lentz removed his goggles and hood. Peering through the windblown snow, he took several steps left, then a few more right. His eyes lifted slowly as he grasped the likelihood of what he had discovered.

"Are you alright, Kyle?" the other scientist asked as he walked up a few feet from behind. "What happened? What did you hit?"

"You're not going to believe this, but I think it's a giant circle," said Dr. Lentz, bending over and wiping the snow from a slightly raised surface on the ground.

He peered again through the snow, trying to see the other edge.

"This thing is huge. The diameter must be at least over a half kilometer wide."

"A circle like a crop circle?" the other scientist asked.

"Maybe—or maybe it's an imprint of something very, very big."

"That's impossible. A team was out here two days ago and didn't report anything about it. How could a circle just appear carved into the ice sheet?"

"I have no idea, but mark it on your GPS. We'll send another team out after the storm. It's going to get bad, so we'd better hurry back."

#

After arriving at the Amundsen-Scott complex, Dr. Lentz dismounted his snowmobile just as the blizzard reached its peak. He approached the huge double garage doors and entered his security code on a keypad. The door retracted vertically, releasing a burst of cold wind and snow into the interior. Followed by his associate, he drove his vehicle into the bay.

The Polheim Station was home to well-equipped biological laboratories and facilities for a wide range of research. The opening of the Amundsen-Scott complex marked the start of new activities in biological sciences in the Antarctic, including scuba diving and other experiments conducted in the facility throughout the year. Meteorological research using satellite data intercepted at the ground station also continued year round. A transitory summer population of scientists and support staff reached Polheim by aircraft flying from the Falkland Islands. The station was equipped with a 900-meter, crushed rock runway, with an associated hangar and fuel storage facility. Fieldwork was concentrated in the summer months from November until March. Once in the field, the parties traveled using skidoos and sledges for up to four months.

#

Dr. Lentz and his associate unloaded their gear and headed for the sleeping quarters.

"What are you going to put in the report?" his associate asked.

"First, I'm going to contact Frank Halverson at the USGS National Center to see if we can get somebody down here to see what that thing is."

He looked at his watch.

"Matter of fact, I think I'll call him right now. I'll see you in the mess hall in about thirty minutes."

As Dr. Lentz headed toward the communication center, the radio operator interrupted him.

"What is it, Radar?" he asked him.

"Sir, you have a message from the Virginia National Center."

Radar handed him a piece of paper.

"Looks like a C-130 out of Port Stanley Airport will be here tomorrow and we're supposed to hand over all operations on a temporary basis to a Colonel Schomberg," said the operator.

Dr. Lentz quickly scanned the communicae.

"How many teams we got out right now, Harry?"

"None . . . Wesley and his team returned this morning just before the storm blew in."

"Good. Nobody leaves the complex until the plane arrives."

"Is there a problem, sir?" the operator asked.

"No . . . it's just a precaution. We found something in the ice when we were setting up more sensors out on the ridge. The military must have spotted it also, so they're sending in a team to investigate. Notify Halverson right away."

The turboprop transport arrived at night during a snowstorm two days later. As the plane touched down the propellers kicked up more snow, making the pilot's landing difficult. Although the weather wasn't conducive for the task, Colonel Schomberg ordered his men to unload the vehicles and other equipment. The modified Hercules C-130 slowly lowered its huge rear door. Dressed in white parkas with thermal trousers, nine civilians disembarked. They stood at the back of the aircraft while men wearing camouflaged clothing removed equipment from the plane's cargo area. Used for carrying personnel and towing sledges of up to eight tons, a Sno-cat cautiously eased down the ramp. After reaching the edge, it's one hundred seventy-horse power engine roared as the vehicle's tracks gripped the ice. Doctor Lentz went to welcome the team.

"Get that equipment into bay eight. It's going to be a rough night," he yelled over the howling wind.

"Dr. Lentz?"

"Yes."

"I'm Colonel Schomberg. Can I speak to you privately?"

"Sure thing Colonel—right this way. Radar, make sure the equipment is secure in bay eight."

"Yes sir."

The colonel followed the scientist through the bay doors, down a narrow corridor and into the main complex.

"My office is just over here."

Dr. Lentz took off his coat and quickly removed a box of charts from the seat of a chair. A miniature basketball rim with netting hung from a file cabinet with a wastebasket underneath. Wads of paper littered the area, evidence of inaccurate targeting. The scientist tried sweeping the balls of paper in a pile with his feet.

"Have a seat, Colonel. Sorry about the mess—we had to let the housekeeper go. You know . . . cut-backs and all that."

Colonel Schomberg looked straight-faced.

"Okay then, what can I do for you?"

The scientist sat his desk.

"Dr. Lentz, I'll get right to the point. The thing you found out on the ice is a matter of national security. Nobody will ever know it ever existed."

"Why not?"

"That's top secret."

"It's alien, isn't it?"

"What makes you say that?"

"Is it?"

"I'm not at liberty to say."

"The world deserves to know, Colonel. If there's concrete evidence that we're not alone, the world should know about it."

"And how do you think they would respond to that knowledge Dr. Lentz? Will there be dancing in the streets of every city? Would countries celebrate the fact that a race of beings exists that is more powerful than they are? Or on the other hand, would the people of this planet suddenly realize that they are as insignificant in the scheme of things as a colony of ants? Have you ever witnessed or experienced chaos, doctor? I don't mean the confusion as a result of your checking account being overdrawn or the anxiety you feel from missing a connecting flight at the airport. I mean real chaos. Because of people like you, six billion people just found out their God doesn't exist. So what's left to have faith in? Let me guess . . . scientists like you. You people never cease to amaze me. Under the guise of truth, you think you're making the world a better place while destroying the very foundations on which civilization rest. You pretend you're above it all. As a scientist, you assume you know what's best for the rest of us. I can give you a thousand examples where members of your little elitist club have invented or discovered something that supposedly would improve the standard of living but ended up killing people or slowly destroying the planet. So spare me the people have a right to know speech, Dr. Lentz. What you really mean is that your pompous profession has a right to tell them whether it's good for them or not."

"It's the people's choice."

"Not today it isn't."

The colonel pulled a large envelope from inside his coat and tossed it on Dr. Lentz's desk. Uneasy, the scientist stared at it for a moment. He raised his eyes slowly. Colonel Schomberg's stare sent a chill down his spine.

"What is this?" he asked, picking the envelope up.

The colonel didn't respond. Dr. Lentz opened the packet and removed the contents.

"What the hell is this?"

"My men and I are going to the site tomorrow to destroy all evidence of the imprint. Your job is to keep your people confined to the complex the entire time. There's a piece of classified space debris in the ice. Use that as your cover story. Do we understand each other, doctor?"

"You can't do this! How did you get pictures of my family?

"I think we're done here."

Chapter Six
Inuit Village Winter Camp

The roads were unpaved and hideously furrowed by water drainage. Scarce vegetation consisted of moss and scattered blades of grass. Water, ice and rock made up most of the landscape. A small village of a few hundred people, the terrain was barren and desolate. Most houses stood on raised posts above ground with the lower area covered with plywood. A huge fuel tank in the center of the village was in frightful disrepair. The most widely dispersed group in the world still leading a partly aboriginal way of life, most Inuit tribes hardly followed the ancient ways anymore. The old shaman's clan was one of the last that did.

Winter brought limited hours of daylight and plummeting temperatures. The ice fields reformed quickly. When they were solid enough, hunters, like polar bears, set out after the seals. Five young men and Kanut, the shaman's grandson, met at one of the four community freezers near the village center. Containing fish, caribou and seal, they arranged and rearranged its contents in preparation for a successful hunt.

"How did you convince your grandfather to let you go hunting?" one of the boys asked Kanut.

"He doesn't know I'm going," he replied, dragging a flat of caribou steaks across the frozen floor.

He pushed it into a corner then sat on top of it.

"Since my parents passed away five years ago, he's been overprotective. He won't let me grow up. Just the other day he gave me this."

He removed a necklace decorated with four, small, ivory polar bears and handed the talisman to the boy.

"He says it will befriend the sea mother that lives in the souls of all animals and protect me from evil spirits."

"It's nice, but will it guarantee a good hunt?" the boy asked, smiling.

Kanut stared at the charms for a moment.

"No, but it reminds me of my heritage and who I am. You guys go on without me. I won't dishonor my grandfather by going hunting without his blessing."

He put on his caribou skin parka and headed home.

#

The Inuit that followed the old ways built superb shelters. Pit houses, made of dirt, timber, and sod protected them from the harsh environment. They lived on the village fringes and were careful not to taint traditional ways with the progressive.

Kanut's grandfather, the old shaman, sat next to a small fireplace dug into the dwelling's wall. With ravenous appetites, the fires licked at fresh offerings. Blue and white flames danced. While on the walls, shadows fluttered.

"Kanut, come sit and warm yourself next to the fire. I have a story, told to me by my father and his father's father, and his father before him." said the shaman.

"A great many hundred winters ago, the great Sea Mother spirit created the world. First she made the fishes, then the land animals, and last of all, man. In the beginning, the animals were alike in power. No one knew which should be food for others and which should be food for Man. Sea Mother told them to meet in one place so that Man may give each its rank and power. The animals all met together one evening, when the sun was set, to wait overnight for the coming of Man the next morning. The sea spirit commanded Man to make bows and arrows, as many as there were animals, and to give the longest one to the animal that was to have the most power, and the shortest to the one, which should have least power. Therefore, he did. After nine nights, his work ended and the bows and arrows, which he had made, were very many. The animals, being together, went to sleep, so they might be ready to meet man the next morning. However, Fox was cunning. He was cunning above all the beasts.

Fox wanted the longest bow and the greatest power so he could have all the other animals for his meat. He decided to stay awake all night, so that he would be first to meet Man in the morning. So he laughed to himself, stretched his nose out on his paw, and pretended to sleep.

"About midnight he began to be sleepy. He had to walk around the camp and scratch his eyes to keep them open. He grew sleepier, so that he had to skip and jump about to keep awake. But he made so much noise, he awakened some of the other animals. When the morning star came up, he was too sleepy to keep his eyes open any longer. He took two little sticks, sharpened them at the ends, and propped open his eyelids. Then he felt safe. He watched the morning star with his nose stretched along his paws, and fell asleep. The sharp sticks pinned his eyelids fast together. The morning star rose rapidly into the sky. The birds began to sing. The animals woke up and stretched themselves, but still Fox lay fast asleep.

"When the sun rose, the animals went to meet Man. He gave the longest bow to Polar Bear, so he had the greatest power. The second longest, he gave to Snow Lion. Others he gave to the other animals, giving all but the last to Frog. However, the shortest one was left. Man cried out, what animal have I missed? Then the animals began to look about and found Fox fast asleep, his eyelids pinned together. All the animals began to laugh. They jumped upon Fox and danced upon him. Then they led him to Man, still blinded. Man pulled out the sharp sticks and gave him the shortest bow of all. It would hardly shoot an arrow farther than a foot. All the animals laughed, but Man took pity on Fox because he was now weaker even than Frog. So at his request, Sea Mother gave him cunning, ten times more than before, so that he was cunning above all animals in the world. Therefore, Fox was friendly to Man and his children, and did many things for them."

He pointed toward the back of the shelter.

"Go to the window and tell me what you see."

Kanut walked to the back room and looked out. A white artic fox sat a few hundred yards away in the snow. Motionless, it stared back at him.

"It's a fox, Grandfather."

Kanut continued watching the fox and the fox watched him.

"Tomorrow we must journey to the spirit caves," said his grandfather.

#

After an arduous six-day trek, the old shaman and his grandson arrived at snow-covered mountains where the caves of the ancestors served as a meeting place with the spirit world. With the help of a staff made of mammoth tusk, he slowly walked up the rocky frozen path followed by his grandson. After entering the mouth of the cave, Kanut grabbed an unlit torch made of sealskin and whale blubber, then ignited it. Several hundred feet into the opening, and through numerous cobwebs, they came to a large chamber. The fire revealed a damp cold place filled with prehistoric drawings, symbols and hieroglyphs. Representations of mammoths, tigers, antelope and paintings of prehistoric beasts decorated the near wall and ceiling. Writings in the Inuit language and other foreign wording were evident throughout. Near the middle of the cavern lay a group of stones, eight in the outer circle and four in an inner circle. In the middle of the four large stones stood a platform with symbols located on the top and sides. Kanut helped his grandfather to the middle of the circle. From there, the old shaman slowly walked up two stairs onto the platform and put his hand on top of an altar. He pulled a small cloth from the pocket of his coat, wiped the dust from a small statue, and placed it on top of the pedestal. The shaman closed his eyes, and began to chant ancient and sacred words.

"*Ajugakangitok tonrar sivudlit kollangorpok. Takungartut tuyurmiangoyok. Tuktu, tarralikitak, kelalogak, krearnartok, nanuk mianersiwok nikpartok. Aksarnerk ikkumayok. Tatkresiwok kraumayok erkpakpok . . ."*

After a short time, he opened his eyes and proclaimed, "Sivudlit tonrars. The ancestors are coming."

Kanut retrieved provisions from the sled. Outside, violent winds picked up loose snow making anything more than eight feet away almost invisible. Anticipating worsening conditions, he removed the dog team from their harnesses and took them inside. They walked about sniffing and marking the floor. Kanut removed ten long rods from beneath the freight sled. He tied each to the toboggan with caribou hide, and then hammered them into the frozen ground, securing it. After several trips outside, Kanut and his grandfather waited.

The shaman awakened to bits of rock and soil hitting the cave floor. He looked at his grandson who slept a few feet from where he lay. The altar on the platform glowed, slightly illuminating the dark and cold cavern. He removed two beautifully carved walrus tusks and a small, caribou skin-covered drum from a basket Kanut had carried in earlier. A silver colored object hovered above the altar, changing shape and brightness. The shaman beat the drum and began chanting.

"Anernerk sivudlit niovgroyok tikitpok, anernerk sivudlit niovgroyok tikitpok, tuyurmiangoyok, kiblariktok sivudlit, kiblariktok sivudlit anernerk sivudlit niovgroyok tikitpok, anernerk sivudlit niovgroyok tikitpok, tuyurmiangoyok, kiblariktok sivudlit, kiblariktok sivudlit—"

The intensity of the object grew, causing bigger pieces of cavern to collapse. The commotion woke Kanut. He sat up quickly, stared at the entity for a moment, and then at his grandfather. Embedded in the walls, previously hidden stained stones lit up and glimmered. The eight outer stones and the four inner stones glowed with increasing brightness, causing Kanut to shield his eyes. Seemingly in a trance, his grandfather was oblivious to the spectacle transpiring around them. Kanut grabbed him by the shoulders and shook him gently.

"Grandfather."

The old shaman didn't respond. He shook him more forcefully.

"Grandfather!" said Kanut a bit louder. "Grandfather, we have to get out. The cave is collapsing . . . Grandfather!"

As quickly as the phenomenon began, it ended. The object disappeared.

Chapter Seven
COMTAC

After exploring the perimeter and surrounding area of an extraordinary and unexpected structure deep in the Sunda Trench, the Pegasus finally broke the surface. The Argo opened her rear recovery bay, welcoming the submersible.

"Docking indicators show green. Pegasus secured, sir."

"Good job, gentlemen. STANCE—run full diagnostic on the Pegasus, download images and upload to SATCOM3 authorization fox delta, bravo, bravo, niner," said Captain Bonar.

"Debriefing in one hour," he announced over the ship's intercom.

Doctor Geraldo climbed out of the deep-water submersible.

"There's some sort of structure down there," she smiled. "We got great pictures; lots of video of part of it. It's unbelievable."

A technician connected the interface immobilizers to the vehicle.

"What do you think it is?" he asked.

"I don't know, but it's old—very old," replied Geri.

"Too bad the remote video converters were down. We could've seen it real-time," said the technical officer. "We'll have it up and running by tomorrow."

With the computer deck being the brain, communications and tactical was the heart of the Argo. It pumped the information gathered by the AI throughout the vessel and if necessary, anywhere in the world.

"Captain Bonar, were having problems interfacing Comtac video with the available ports," said an engineer.

"I swear this ship has more problems than an Apollo Saturn V rocket. Put it on the list, Teri, and inform Doctor Nashikato."

"Yes sir," she said.

"And tell him to switch to secondary auxiliary systems in conference hall A8991," yelled the captain as he walked away.

That evening the AI loaded the video footage.

With S.T.A.N.C.E. as the commentator, the audience sat quietly as the images ran on a large wall monitor.

"Steep relief of the seafloor and evidences of collapse and slope failure caused by the earthquakes have been found by seafloor observation. Following seafloor observations near the epicenter suggest the place of collapse and slope failure, and traveling of collapsed sediment to deep water. Turbid water at downstream in a submarine canyon was found. No turbid water at upstream in the submarine canyon was found. A number of collapsed reliefs, especially angular-edged surfaces where ruptures took place was found. Abundant open fissures in the terrace were found. Fissures were not filled with sand, which could be transported by ripple current. The acoustic investigation detected a possible ragged relief. The steep slopes at up and middle streams of the canyon were covered with falling rocks and displaced sediments. No trace of organisms, and benthic creatures were found in the bottom surface."

The communication officer stood at the front of the room near the monitor with a remote red laser pointer. She pressed a button on it, stopping the digital recording.

"The image of the counter bottom left is the depth marker," she explained. "Below that is the pressure indicator, the water temperature and the oxygen timer. There's multiple applications associated with the system. Several have been declassified to assist you."

She pressed another button on the remote.

"STANCE, locate, playback file eight two Hilo Niner Beta."

Surprisingly, the AI responded vocally.

"File located. Play back in progress."

"STANCE?" one of the members asked.

"Strategic Tactical and Navigation Communications Environment," the technical officer responded.

The digital images began again.

"This is the Pegasus at four thousand, two hundred eighty-five feet. And this," said the officer, looking at the remote and pressing another button, "this is a classified feature."

A square image appeared in the upper right-hand corner of the screen.

"It's an Electromagnetic Field Modulator Receptor. For every 33 feet down traveled, one more atmospheres, 14.7 per square inch push down on us. For example, at 66 feet, the pressure equals 44.1 psi, and at 99 feet, the pressure equals 58.8 psi. At twenty-six thousand plus feet below the surface, the water pressure should be way above what you see here."

She pointed at the pressure counter again. Sounds of murmurings overtook the room.

"And this, ladies and gentlemen, is the partial object captured by the Pegasus. The computer is able to extrapolate the incomplete image into a full representation within an eighty-seven percent probability."

"So what you're saying is that the pressure from that depth should be higher? Maybe the sensors are malfunctioning?" one of the oceanographers interrupted.

Annoyed, the lieutenant moved a few steps toward the scientist, switching the remote from her left to right hand.

"STANCE."

"Yes, Lieutenant Mitchell," the technological marvel responded perfunctory.

"Run diagnostic systems Zulu Delta five five Delta."

"Diagnostic completed. All subsurface systems operating within specified parameters."

Lieutenant Mitchell retreated.

"As you can see, there's nothing wrong with the ship's equipment."

Sensing his officer's indignation, the captain of the Argo stepped in.

"Gentlemen—and ladies, we can only achieve a successful mission with the cooperation of both military and civilian agencies."

"Mission? First, they think we need water pressure 101 and now a mission?" a scientist uttered.

Dr. Geraldo gave her a slight jab with an elbow.

"Now—there's something down there and STANCE isn't able to locate the Z point because of unidentifiable interference. Therefore, I suggest everyone remain professional and do their job," said Captain Bonar. "Dr. Geraldo, please accompany me to Ops. Lieutenant, please continue."

Followed by Geri, Captain Bonar headed toward the operations deck.

#

"Dr. Geraldo, this is a very serious and delicate situation we have here. From what I hear, the Department of Defense asked for your assistance based on your expertise and experience. You haven't mentioned this to your team, have you?"

"No, of course not," she replied.

"Good. Let me remind you that this is a matter of national security. Were you briefed on the item?"

"Yes," replied Geri.

"Excellent. You have clearance to discuss the material with your people."

He handed her a folder with "Confidential Top Secret" stamped on it.

"Doctor, you are not to discuss certain specifics of this operation. Is that understood?"

"Yes sir."

"You are not to discuss the item or the significance of said item. Is this understood?"

"Yes sir."

"Look, Dr. Geraldo, I know your father is an admiral in the United States Navy. I don't know the real reason why or how you were chosen for this job, but I do know I have my orders—and those orders are to assist you in a recovery operation. It's clear my people don't want your people here, and I happen to think this is a military matter and should be handled strictly by the military. So let's try and do the job, and get back to port as quickly as possible."

"Captain Bonar, my father had no influence on my being chosen for this mission, so back off and let my people and I do what we were sent here to do," she responded angrily.

"Okay Doctor . . . fine. Tomorrow several of your people and mine will take the submersibles to the site. We'll be looking for an entrance to get into the main structure and hopefully locate the source once we're there. My men have already been briefed, so take the declassified material and bring your people up to speed."

"Yes sir, right away, sir."

She gave him a sarcastic salute. Brushing against him as she left, Geri headed back to her quarters.

"STANCE."

"Yes, Dr. Geraldo."

"Locate Professor Tanaka and Doctor Hanrahan."

"Professor Tanaka and Doctor Hanrahan are located in the conference hall, D deck two," replied the AI.

#

In the conference room the presentation continued. Scientists and military personnel sat awestruck at the images shown on the monitor. The enormous structure, as much as could be seen, was a mixture of cultures. The head of Brahma, the Hindu god of creation and one of the Trimurti stood guard high above a hidden entrance while the entire construction seemed to rest on the feet of Zeus. Giant pillars ran across the large steps.

"Notice the areas of the structure similar to the Classical and Hellenistic eras," Professor Tanaka pointed out.

"Yes, and the Ajanta caves of India also may have had some influence on the builders," replied Doctor Hanrahan. "Interesting that the two periods are a millennia apart, isn't it?"

"I think there's more here than we've been told," one of the oceanographers added.

Geri walked into the lounged.

"Lieutenant Mitchell, will you excuse us?"

"Yes ma'am," she replied and left.

Geri stood at the front of her team near the monitor.

"STANCE—pause play. Okay, ladies and gentlemen, we've been given clearance for the full extent of what we're up against. About fifty-three years ago, there were a number of experiments called the Rainbow and the Montauk Projects. In the fall of 1943, a U.S. Navy destroyer was rendered invisible and teleported from Philadelphia, Pennsylvania, to Norfolk, Virginia, in an incident known as the Philadelphia Experiment. The Montauk Project was to be an elite black project investigating paranormal, psychic, and unconventional sciences. It was to include the most intelligent respected scientists in the world using the most sophisticated advanced computer equipment available. The Montauk project turned out to become a huge project branching off into many other smaller projects, including mind control, telepathy, teleportation and time travel.

"Wait—you think the structure is extraterrestrial, don't you?" a team member asked.

Geri continued.

"I'm not going to go into any greater detail of those experiments, but I'll tell you guys this—: What we do here today has repercussions beyond our understanding. What some of you may witness in the next couple of days may test your perception of reality and the laws of physics. And now I'd like to introduce Doctor Nashikato, expert in Condensed Matter Physics and Spatial Multiphase theory from the Ames Laboratory."

"Thank you, Dr. Geraldo. We'll be attempting to penetrate an outpost tomorrow. An outpost built millennia ago. If you look at the monitor, you'll see what we expect to find."

The AI retrieved a picture of a temple and superimposed it on the image taken on the dive.

"We think the structure is a mixture of several cultures. For instance, Mayan, Egyptian, Greek, and many more we couldn't identify. Our job is to find an entrance to the structure and explore it. A military team will accompany us for security purposes. Are there any questions?"

"Why weren't we informed of this from the beginning?" one of the oceanographers asked.

"How long has the government known about this?" another asked before Dr. Nashikato could answer.

"Please, please one at a time. A DOD satellite discovered the structure ten years ago after an underwater earthquake in the area. Most of you have been kept in the dark because it's considered a matter of national security."

"National Security? What would an out-of-place sunken temple have to do with National Security?" asked an archaeologist.

Nashikato took a deep breath.

"Unfortunately, there are still some aspects I'm not at liberty to discuss. However, it probably will become clear once the structure is explored."

"That's bullshit," the oceanographer said in disgust. "You get us out here on false pretenses, then tell us only part of the reason why? Then you use National Security as a pretext to keep us in the dark? I won't go."

"That's your choice," Dr. Nashikato responded. "Is there anybody else that has come to the same decision?"

The conference hall fell silent as the participants looked around the room at one another.

"Good. I have in my hand copies of the nondisclosure agreements everyone signed at Yokota Air Force Base. Attached is an addendum."

He laid them on the table.

"We launch tomorrow morning."

#

On the bridge, Captain Bonar, Lieutenant-Commander Tarkenston and Sergeant Davidson, the Special Ops team leader, scanned the horizon with binoculars.

"LC."

"Yes sir," answered the lieutenant-commander.

"Run another full diagnostic on the Pegasus and Cerberus. I want to make sure they are ready for tomorrow's deployment."

"Yes sir."

"Captain, we picked up a vessel on an intercept course," said a Comtac radar operator through the intercom.

"What kind of vessel?"

"Indications are it's the Indonesian Coast Guard Cutter Guntur," he replied.

"STANCE, set counter measures and activate Dead Star protocols," ordered Captain Bonar.

"What if they already have a fix on our position?" Sergeant Davidson asked.

"Then we'll look like a disappearing echo. Keep an eye on the Guntur and notify me if she changes heading, Mac. LC—I want you to head up the Pegasus and Lieutenant Mitchell will pilot the Cerberus. Mitch will deploy the SPECIAL OPS team and return. Lieutenant-Commander, you'll escort the civilian team and remain on site as a liaison between the military and Geri's people. Sergeant Davidson, I'm sure you know your orders—provide security and assist in recovery."

"Yes sir," the sergeant acknowledged.

"The Cerberus will attempt to find a point of entry. People—I don't need to remind you what's at stake here."

The next morning, the crew prepared to launch the submersibles. Several malfunctions caused the ship's technical engineers to temporarily shut down and reboot all systems overnight. Support aircraft from Diego Garcia protected the vulnerable vessel as she sat soaking up the moonlight for a few dark and lonely hours. By dawn, the Argo and STANCE, the AI, were fully functional. Scientific equipment and other supplies were loaded onto the submersibles in anticipation of the major operation.

Geri's team went over procedures, then checked and re-checked delicate gear. They divided into two groups, those with archeological and physics expertise and those well versed in earth sciences. The men in charge of protecting them gathered ordinances and assembled weapons. Dr. Nashikato dispensed the team prototype military fatigues.

"They're the latest from the Pentagons Advance Research Agency," he said proudly.

To the casual observer, the clothing was unremarkable. However, the optical camouflage fatigues employed thousands of micro-cameras to photograph surroundings once every one point four seconds. It then transmitted the images to a micro-processing unit, displaying it on billions of flexible, organic, light-emitting nano-screens.

With the SPECIAL OPS unit on board, the Cerberus was the first to launch.

"STANCE, initiate communications protocols," Lieutenant Mitchell requested.

"Initiating communication protocols," STANCE responded.

"I'm reading you nice and clear. You've got green across the board," the communications officer replied.

"Initiating launch sequence."

In the belly of the Argo, massive doors retracted. The submersible entered the ocean's deep.

"Cerberus away, sir," the operations officer announced.

"STANCE—auto tracking mode only," Captain Bonar requested.

"Auto tracking engaged."

"Captain, we've got a red light on GLRC. SRC and all other communication systems still operable," said the Com officer.

"I need long-range communications, Mr. McDonald. We can't talk to the outside world without it. Run a diagnostic on it, Mac."

Captain Bonar walked a few feet to video radar operations, leaned over and put his hand on the shoulder of one of his men.

"Guys, I want you both to keep a sharp lookout for anything. Who knows what's down there or what we may face. Kirk, give me a picture upfront on monitors four, six, A12 and A13 with all parameters, including laser, VHF, and ambient noise imaging. Walter?"

"A.I. signal processing green across the board, sir."

"She's a remarkable piece of technology," remarked Dr. Geraldo.

"Aye, that she is ma'am," the technical officer responded.

"Is the Pegasus prepped and ready?" Captain Bonar asked.

"Pegasus ready to deploy."

"Dr. Geraldo, if you'll get down to the launch bay . . . Mac, give me an ETA to the Z point."

"At present speed, seventeen minutes, sir."

"Seventeen minutes? How can a submersible descend that quickly?" a scientist asked.

"That's classified, sir," said the technical officer.

Captain Bonar pressed a communications pad.

"LC, what's your status?"

"Awaiting Launch Green, sir," he responded.

#

Aboard the Cerberus and in the rear of the craft, the six-man SPECIAL OPS and Beach Jumper unit checked and rechecked their gear.

"Listen up, ladies. This one's by the book. We have very little Intel, so we're going in blind. Consider the situation hostile until otherwise advised. If conditions become unreceptive, we spit into two teams. Danny Boy and T.J., you're with Dickerson; Harris, you and Tank are with me.

STANCE—initiate SPECIAL OPS team protocol authorization—Sierra, Willow, Alpha, eight, four, four, eight, Alpha. Initiate com to com and video."

"Communications and video green across the board, Sergeant Davidson," the communications officer replied.

Lieutenant Mitchell sat upfront piloting.

"STANCE, give me a heads up display on currents and temperature and calculate vector to Z point, load and display."

The information appeared translucent in the center of the forward geodesic dome.

"Apply stabilizers thirty percent; continue to monitor and adjust automatically. Sergeant Davidson—we've got turbulence coming up from deep sea ocean currents. It may get a little rough from here on out. Five minutes till Z point," Lieutenant Mitchell announced through her headset.

"Copy that," Sergeant Davidson responded.

Dickerson, one of the team members recited the SEAL code.

"Loyalty to country, team and teammates . . ."

The other soldiers joined in.

"Serve with honor and integrity on and off the battlefield, ready to lead, ready to follow, never quit, take responsibility for your actions and the actions of your teammates, excel as warriors through discipline and innovation, train for war, fight to win, defeat our nation's enemies, earn your trident every day."

"Alright ladies, put your game faces on," Sergeant Davidson barked.

T.J. slapped Danny Boy on the back.

"Rock and Roll time, D Boy!"

He stood up.

"Let's get busy, J!"

They executed their secret six-step handshake. Tank removed a double-barreled handgun from a holster strapped to his leg. He had modified it to fire shotgun ammo.

"What's that for?" Dickerson asked.

"I call her the Oracle," he answered, loading the weapon. "Just think of her as the answer to the unknown."

Lieutenant Mitchell's voice echoed through their headsets.

"One minute to target."

"Copy that," Captain Bonar replied. "Mitch, you should see an opening near the south wall."

"Yes sir," replied Lieutenant Mitchell. "STANCE, go to one-half thrusters and deploy AUV's full array. Captain, we're out the pipe, launching autonomous underwater vehicles—optimum packages."

"Copy that. Pegasus, stand-by," radioed the captain.

"Pegasus standing by."

#

Dr. Geraldo addressed her team of experts. Mendel Hanrahan, PhD, an Anthropological Archaeologist from Colombia University; John Stolte, PhD, Yale University, Biologist, Maritime Archaeology expert; Professor Patricia Rosenbaum, Theoretical Astrophysics and Applied Sciences, Oxford University; and Professor Harry Tanaka, Mathematical Engineer, ancient architecture expert, from Tokyo University, all were chosen after extensive background checks.

"Everyone stay alert and don't take any unnecessary risks. Sergeant Davidson and his men will be providing security, so follow their lead. If there is anything that they deem unsafe or hostile, you are to follow their instructions to the letter. Depending on the situation and the structure's layout, we may need to split into two teams. Are there any questions?"

No one answered.

"Excellent. Good luck."

Chapter Eight
Hotel de la Paix Geneva

Sitting majestically by the shore of Lake Geneva, with sweeping views of snow-capped Mont Blanc, the historic and prestigious Hotel de la Paix Geneva offered a unique environment where tradition and period elegance mingle harmoniously with contemporary charm. With regal elegance above Geneva's lakeside embankment, it exuded a rare allure, even by European standards.

David arrived at the hotel around six-thirty. He pulled up to the entrance and handed his car keys to the valet.

"Good evening, Dr. Woodall," Stefan, the concierge greeted him with his familiar smile. "Back for a little R &R?"

David hadn't seen him since November ninety-eight, the last time he was in Switzerland to work on a project with a professor from MIT.

"Stefan, my good friend," greeted David, reaching out to shake his hand. "How's the family? Katrina, what is she eleven, twelve now? How's the wife?"

"Ahhhh, the family couldn't be better, my friend," he responded, grasping Dr. Woodall's hand with a solid grip. "Katrina, yes she's twelve now and almost as tall as I. Well, the misses—let's just say she's still the most beautiful woman in the world. And you, David—how's life treating you? When did you get in?"

"Life? Life is treating me just fine, thank you. My plane landed last night and I had to be at the lab early this morning. Arbete för förmiddag I på en projektera."

"Very good. I see your grasp of the Swedish language has improved. And what task have you been assigned this time, old friend?"

David put his hand on his shoulder.

"Stefan, if I told you I'd have to kill you," he replied jokingly. "It's the same old story. I get a call asking if I'm available at a certain date for a certain undertaking. I sign confidentially documents and am sworn to secrecy."

They chuckled and walked into the hotel.

After stepping into the extraordinary galleried lobby, the Hotel de la Paix delivered the ultimate in sensory pleasure. Greeted by jeweled chandeliers amid subtle blends of decor old and new, the entrance was an exquisite introduction to the luxury beyond. Proudly embarking upon its third century as Geneva's premier boutique hotel, it successfully preserved its rich heritage.

"And still no wife, Dr. Woodall?"

"No wife yet, but I do see someone about twice a month; it's complicated. By the way, tell Lovisa nice work setting me up with Kia last time I was in town. I found it odd a woman with her looks would be interested in me with a bar full of rich and eligible men available. She was quite something. We must have talked at least an hour about her breast implants. She even offered to show them to me."

"And of course, you declined?"

"Well, after a couple of drinks, she decided it was her duty as a citizen of Sweden to show them to the patrons and I while dancing on a table."

"Oh my," said Stefan, blushing.

"Best time I've ever had," David lied.

Embarrassed by the ordeal, he'd walked out of the bar as soon as the woman took off her blouse.

"Good for you."

Stefan knew that the woman's behavior had made him uncomfortable.

"I'll make sure Lovisa gets your approval before she sets you up with a date next time," said Stefan with his familiar smile.

The men shook hands again and David headed toward the elevators.

The hotel was an excellent location for meetings and conferences in Geneva, one of Europe's most significant business cities. During his stay, several conventions were in progress.

As the elevator doors opened, several people exited. A lone female stood in the rear corner. Petite with a slightly beige and yellow undertone complexion, her eyes burned pastel green. Bistre shoulder-length hair partially covered her face. She wore a custom-tailored, tropical wool suit with two-button fastenings. Her matching full-length bias skirt, fully lined, fit perfectly. Emilio Pucci pumps with piping trim decorated small and unquestionably well-pampered feet.

David hesitated for a moment, forcing himself to enter. She moved past him, pressing the button for floor nine. The smell of her perfume filled the enclosure. David took a deep breath, quietly inhaling the exquisite fragrance. As the elevator came to a stop, she stood next to him, looked into his eyes and smiled. He returned it with a sheepish grin as she exited. David exhaled, then pushed floor fourteen.

The modern designed guestroom featured a flat-screen satellite television and a complimentary mini bar. Contemporary furnishings blended with the period design of the hotel.

After taking a shower and checking his email, he headed to the Nobel bar for a meal.

"Ska dig sammanfogar oss för matställeherrn. Will you be joining us for dinner, sir?" the maître d' asked.

A technician from the lab sat at the bar having a cocktail.

"Dr. Woodall," he called and motioned David over to him.

"Inget inte ikväll. Tacka dig. Thank you, but I'll be having something at the bar."

The Nobel bar and restaurant featured an exclusive selection of vintage port wines, rare liqueurs, cigars and brandies. The mahogany floor, fireplace, and luxuriously comfortable sofas and armchairs made it a pleasurable place to enjoy light snacks. A pianist subtly entertained five nights a week and various live bands sometimes livened the evening proceedings.

"Dr. Woodall, would you like to join me for a drink?"
"Sure," David replied, sitting down.
He ordered a glass of wine.
"Chteau La Mondotte, please."
"I read your paper on dimensions and was wondering if you could help me understand the theory."
"Well," replied Dr. Woodall. "It's not an easy concept to comprehend. Let's see."
He scanned the room.
"Look around the bar. What do you see?"
"I see people, chairs and tables, among other things."
"Well—those objects take up space in our dimension."
David held up two glasses.
"Now what do you see? Look between the spaces of the glasses."
"Nothing—I don't see anything but empty space."
"Think of it as this. The glasses are taking up space in our dimension, where the space between them represents another dimension. From another dimension, an object occupies the space between the glasses and no objects can occupy the space you currently see."
"Huh?"
"Do you have a piece of paper and something to write with?" David asked.
The technician pulled a receipt and a pen from his shirt pocket.
"Sure, here you go."
Dr. Woodall took the paper and drew a large circle, inserting a dot in the middle. He then connected the circle with lines leading to the dot.
"Look at the point carefully. Is it at the end of a tunnel or the top of a cone?"
"I see a wheel with spokes," answered the technician.
"Your brain sees it as an object on a two-dimensional surface. In order to really understand my theory, you'll have to train your mind to see objects as they relate to space. Here you go."

David handed the technician his pen and paper.

"Keep it. Pull it out every once in a while and take a good look at it. In about two or three months you'll start to see the unseen around you in everything. The trick is to train your mind to think dimensionally. Then, you'll be able to see the invisible."

Completely mystified, the technician stood up, shook Dr. Woodall's hand, said thank you, good night, and then left.

David took a sip of his wine. He wondered if he had overexplained the concept. The technician probably had no background or training in Quantum Physics, yet he spoke to him as if he'd been giving a lecture at Oxford.

There I go again, he thought to himself.

He took another drink as his demons sat next to him.

"You don't belong here. Nobody knows what you've been through. They don't understand you like we do," they whispered.

In school, several teachers sheltered David because of his intellect. They felt his anguish, saw his potential, and tried to cultivate it. Other instructors were uncaring and unsympathetic. They'd seen it all before. Thousands of children with special abilities had sat before them. Abilities, if carefully nurtured, would take them to places most could only imagine. Unable to overcome his family's chaotic environment, he was just another in a long line of students with a wasted cerebral aptitude.

Who was the real David Jason Woodall? Was he the shy unsure individual, a product of his circumstances from long ago, or the confident, articulate and knowledgeable person? David was living in two worlds and struggling to merge them.

"Know thyself. Seek answers to questions not yet asked," he muttered to himself.

He finished his wine and headed back to his room—without dinner.

#

An early morning telephone call woke David. He answered it, trying to sound alert.

"Hello."

His gruffly voice betrayed him.

"David? Did I wake you?"

"Geri?"

He felt a sudden rush of adrenalin. Unable to hide the excitement in his voice, he sat up immediately.

"How's everything going? How did you find me?" he asked.

David and Geri had met when everything was reasonably stable in his life. She was a young and brilliant upstart anthropology student at Yale University and him, a struggling physics major. They had a lot in common. They talked for hours about life, death and everything in between. Both had the same sense of humor, enjoyed beautiful things and new experiences. They became good friends. She knew him. She knew what he was feeling and most of the time knew what he was going to say before he said it. Both fought to overcome the psychological effects of tumultuous childhoods. She felt what he felt. He trusted her.

One night on their way to a local pub where some of his friends hung out, he leaned over the car consol and unexpectedly kissed her. Of course, she was flabbergasted. She had never been kissed that way before and didn't know how she felt about David, at least not romantically. She also had a boyfriend.

"David, you of all people should know I have my ways. I just called to make sure you're doing okay. How are you?"

"I'm doing okay I guess—just busy working on a project. What are you up to these days?"

"I'm aboard a research vessel off the coast of Indonesia," answered Geri.

"From the lack of details, I'm assuming you're working on something for the DOD?"

She knew it was impossible to keep anything from him.

She had never met someone so close to her, so able to see inside her. He was able to touch her soul and she his. From the moment she had met him, she knew there was something there, something beyond a personal connection. She didn't believe in reincarnation, but she felt she knew him before they ever met. Somehow, he was part of her past; the past before her spirit had no vessel; a past where souls roamed through time until the moment arose to reside in the physical realm. David was a familiar soul. He was the calming influence in her life.

"Yeah, but don't tell anybody," she laughed. "Listen, I'm calling because I wanted you to know I'm okay and I missed you."

"Geri, what are you getting ready to do? Where are you exactly?" His heart raced.

"I'm not in any trouble—yet. I'm just kidding. Can't I call to say I miss you without you worrying about me?"

"No. You know how I am. You know I tend to think the worst," said David.

"Well there is no "worst" this time. By the way, the old man told me to tell you hello. Can you meet us in Indonesia at the Inna Dharma Deli Hotel tomorrow; let's say three o'clock local time?"

"Who's going to be there?" asked David.

She knew what he was thinking.

"Just the old man and me," she replied.

"Don't worry, Justino won't be there. We've been having problems lately, so we took a little break from one another. Besides, I couldn't bring him along. He doesn't have clearance for anything involving the Department of Defense."

Chapter Nine
The Commission

"Mr. Yamokoto, have you acquired the artifact?"
"It is in the secured location, Madam."
The woman opened another file.
"Mr. Teller."
She flipped through several pages.
"Have you the Phaistos Disk?"
"The object is in the commission's possession and is currently being studied at the Zurich facility," he answered. "The disc is traditionally dated between 1700-1500 BC. However, some symbols, such as the central flower and the two-container symbol, are indicative of Pharaonic Egypt in the Old Kingdom, but no later. The physical disk surely dates to the second millennium, but we dated some of the forerunner mathematics and symbols on the disk to earlier periods. I recommend further study."
"Good . . . and Professor Chiang."
"Yes Madam."
"What's the status on the Atlantis Ring?"
"It is also at the Zurich facility. The object seems to be paranormal in nature with measurable scientific properties. Current test results shows that it creates a shield that gives the wearer protection from accidents or bad luck. It also augments the ability to tap into one's own intuitive powers and subconscious. Further study is recommended."
Madam pressed a button on the phone unit. A man appeared on a large monitor.
"Doctor Willoughby, are you still there?"
"Yes Madam."
"I've recently received a new and disturbing report on the incident involving Dr. Jamison at Los Alamos."
"The Eclipseso Project?" asked Dr. Willoughby.

"According to eye witnesses, Dr. Jamison ordered activation of the laser injectors even though the synchrotron radiation output was way past critical at one hundred and eighty percent. Even when the environment outside the containment field became compromised, he still increased the magnetic coils and polarized gun output."

"Dr. Jamison was attempting to create a proto-universe by changing the ryhsmonic frequency of certain subatomic particles. Trying to force enough energy together to initiate gravitational collapses . . . any experiment of that nature would surely have its uncertainties and the outcome would be highly unpredictable," said Dr. Willoughby.

"According to the report, he gained access to an experimental particle collider through influence and data manipulation. It seems the good doctor has a habit of putting personal gain above anything else. Keep an eye on him and investigate any request carefully."

"Yes Madam."

She turned the monitor off.

"Mr. Sandoval and Miss Ibaqu—I believe your assignment was the Crystal Skull of Lubaantun."

Pushing his chair back from the long redwood table, Randall Sandoval stood up and spoke first.

"Madam, a lack of necessary resources has hindered retrieval of the object."

"Excuses, Mister Sandoval? I will not tolerate excuses!"

She slammed her fist against the table. Shaken, Mr. Sandoval sat down, shuffled his papers, then nervously put them into his briefcase.

"Miss Ibaqu," Madam spoke sternly, "you are now in charge of the Lubaantun project."

She slid a blue folder down the long table past several people.

"Please go over the file and decide on another to join your team as your assistant."

The Madam motioned to two well-dressed men standing by the door.

"Albert, Sven, please escort Mr. Sandoval off the premises," she said calmly.

They walked over to Mr. Sandoval, each grabbing him by an arm. Surprised, he stood up, knocking his chair over and spilling contents from his briefcase onto the floor. He attempted to retrieve the errant papers, however Albert and Sven wasted no time shoving him toward the glass door. His glasses hanging from one ear, Sandoval readjusted them.

"You can't do this to me. I have a contract. I'll sue. You'll hear from my lawyer. I'll sue!" he yelled.

He swore at the two men as they pushed him into the elevator with four other security officers.

"Miss Ibaqu, is there any other resources you require to complete your task?" the Madam asked.

Miss Ibaqu hands trembled as she timidly shook her head.

"No Madam. I believe I have all the resources I need to successfully recover the Lubaantun Crystal skull," she replied in her East Cushitic accent.

"This organization was not built on maybe or possibly. I suggest you focus on your assignment or suffer the same fate as Mr. Sandoval."

At this, only the sound of silence could be heard. The eight men and women sitting at the table knew what she meant. Mr. Sandoval wasn't seen alive again.

The commission had collected artifacts and relics for centuries. In 118 BC, the king of Numidia died, leaving the crown to his young sons, Hiempsal and Adherbal, jointly with a much older nephew, Jugurtha. Jugurtha arranged the assassination of Hiempsal, while Adherbal fled for his life and appealed to the senate. The Roman Senate decided to create and send a commission to Numidia to divide the kingdom between the two claimants. Jugurtha bribed the commission's leader, who returned to Rome a richer man after awarding the greater and wealthier part of Numidia to him. Later, the commission not only settled disputes between kingdoms and empires, it also collected Christian and other artifacts on the orders of Constantine II and the Emperors thereafter. Zurich was one of many covert facilities operated by the commission.

#

A large black limousine with dark tinted windows drove up to the heavily guarded and fortified gate. Three uniformed men with semiautomatic weapons approached the vehicle while four others stood ready at the entrance. A woman wearing a distinctive uniform stepped from a booth and walked up to the automobile's window.

"Kan jag se dina dokument behaga?"

The limousine's window mechanically retracted. A white gloved hand extended, holding a black passport-like credential. The woman opened the identification document, studied it carefully, and then looked at the driver.

"Förlåta mig herrnen. Översittare förväntades inte till I morgon."

"As you can see, Madam is early. She will have your pretty little head for your incompetence," said the driver.

Uneasy, she stepped backwards and waved the security personnel to lower the suicide barricades, opening the gate.

A pallid two-story facility constructed of masonry load-bearing walls and almost windowless, outwardly, there was nothing particularly exceptional about building LL7. Inside, however, German-born Doctor Hastings Willoughby, who was more of an administrator than a research scientist, headed up a brilliant group of researchers, investigators and technicians. The staff, consisting of multiple nationalities, was loyal and sworn to secrecy. Due to the nature of the subject matter, each individual had signed the standard commission nondisclosure agreement. Being what it was—violating it meant certain demise. Accordingly, the commission compensated their personnel substantially.

Dr. Willoughby met Madam at a door that concealed the genuine characteristics of LL7. He was eager to show off the new security features installed earlier. Upon entering a security code, the door opened into another room. After entering a unique code, another door opened into an elevator that took patrons six hundred feet below the surface to the operations and research facilities.

"Was the Uruguay recovery successful?" Madam questioned Dr. Willoughby.

A woman of roughly fifty-two years of age, she was as equally mysterious as dangerous. Always splendidly dressed, she wore mostly white, often with a fox or minx stole. Madam needed no interpreters. She was talented and spoke over thirty different dialects. Thus, she was a "hands on" type of manager. The commission knew her as a "get it done at any cost" type of executive, which indeed made her dangerous to friend or foe.

"Yes Madam, the artifact was recovered and the subject terminated."

"Who gave orders to terminate Dr. Doyle?" she snapped, grabbing him by the arm.

"It . . . it was unavoidable, Madam," the scientist said fearfully. "Our operatives attempted several times to obtain the item discreetly, but all were unsuccessful."

She grabbed him by the throat.

"What do you mean? What have you done, fool?"

"The final opportunity was to retrieve the object on the plane, Madam," Dr. Willoughby winced.

Polanco—eighteen days earlier

The town of Polanco had only one legitimate airport. Most were a collection of dirt landing strips used by farmers and drug traffickers. With shortened paved runways, the Polanco airfield was capable of servicing planes no larger than the prop variety. It connected passengers to other towns with sufficient facilities and eventually to Montevideo International Airport.

Alvarez drove his truck to a small terminal where planes departed and arrived from various locals. Dr. Doyle got out and removed luggage from the rear of the vehicle, then walked around to the driver's side.

"I'll be in Chicago for about three days. I'll call you when I arrive in Montevideo."

"Okay. Have a good flight, Dr. Doyle."

A mysterious man wearing a straw hat and sunglass stood across the road next to a fruit stand eating an apple. He watched with keen interest as Dr. Doyle headed into the building. Discarding the fruit, the commission operative picked up a backpack and followed.

Inside the terminal, passengers waited in short lines to purchase tickets at the counter. Other patrons awaited the arrival of love ones or friends on incoming flights. A native sat on a chair next to a widow overlooking the runway. He wore a white hat, unsoiled by the local dust. His shirt was clean and nicely pressed; his brown leather boots shined from a recent polishing. Next to him sat a crate containing a rooster, undoubtedly a prized cockfighting possession. He spoke to it periodically, encouraging it for an upcoming competition. His wife and kids sat on opposite sides. The man kissed them goodbye as a voice announced the departing flight to Corrales.

"One ticket to Montevideo," requested Dr. Doyle as he approached the counter. He sat his bag on the floor. The mysterious man stood in line a few customers behind him.

"Sou não dizem ingles," said a ticket agent.

Another agent came over to assist her.

"Sorry, we don't get many Americans in town. How can I help you?"

Exhibiting very little inflection, he spoke English remarkably well for a Uruguayan.

"I'd like a ticket to Montevideo," said Dr. Doyle.

The ticket agent looked at the display, then entered a few strokes on the keyboard.

"There's a flight scheduled for departure in thirty-five minutes. It stops in Paso De Los Toros and Tres Arboles before landing in Montevideo. There's also a flight two days from now on Thursday at 2:00 p.m."

"I'll take the flight today."

"Okay then, that'll be nine hundred and sixty-six pesos," said the agent.

Dr. Doyle removed his wallet and offered him a handful of the local currency. The agent quickly counted it, handing back several bills. He typed more keystrokes, then retrieved a green card expelled from a printer.

"Your ticket, sir. The plane is boarding now."

"Thank you."

Dr. Doyle picked up his bag, then proceeded outside to board the plane. The ticket agent handed the man a large carry-on and a passenger's permit from behind the counter. The operative then followed Doctor Doyle to the tarmac.

Twenty-seven passengers boarded as the twin-engine plane sat outside the small building. Ragged seats and debris decorated the cabin. As he entered, Doctor Doyle paused for moment. A repugnant odor staggered him slightly. He untied a bandana from his neck and placed it over his mouth.

"My god, there were better accommodations on the flight out of Ta-kaw," he mumbled to himself.

He moved to the center of the plane and sat down. Because the seatbelt buckle was missing, Dr. Doyle tied the strap around his waist.

The wind picked up considerably as the plane taxied out to the runway. As it ascended, it shook and swayed from severe turbulence. Nervous, Dr. Doyle bit his lip and cuffed his hands together. The aircraft dropped a hundred feet as several passengers screamed and began to pray. The engines groaned, desperate to overcome strong crosswinds. The plane suddenly corrected its flight and settled in at ten thousand feet. A sigh of relief rang throughout the cabin as passengers kissed crosses and gave thanks.

The commission's operative sat in the rear. He put on a mask, then removed three small canisters from the carry-on bag, releasing an undetectable sleeping agent. Minutes later, twenty-seven passengers lay unconscious. He approached the cockpit door with gun drawn, opened it and ordered the pilot to put the plane on auto. The odorless gas overwhelmed the captain and copilot, unintentionally incapacitating them. The operative went back to the cabin to retrieve the box from Dr. Doyle's bag. He stared at the rooster for a brief moment, unconscious in its crate. It convulsed periodically, a fatality of the unscented murderous vapor. The man strapped on the backpack, opened the plane's door and parachuted out.

#

"The plane crashed? He was supposed to disable the passengers! Were there any survivors or witnesses? Speak fool!"

She slowly removed her hand from his neck. Doctor Willoughby gathered himself.

"No Madam," he choked. "No one survived. All twenty-seven passengers and crew are dead."

"That's very good, Hastings, my dear. Where is the item?" Madam asked.

"It's on level five, the imaging lab, Madam. The technicians are measuring light relating to the electromagnetic spectrum emanating from the artifact."

"How long will the spectroscopy process take?"

"It should be done this afternoon, Madam."

"Should be done?"

"It will be as you wish, Madam," he said, bowing.

In the imaging room, the examination of the box was indeed proceeding. As technicians carried out multi-spectral imaging scans, it emitted a strange blue glow and changed its shape to an irregular polyhedron.

Chapter Ten
Encounter

Aboard the Argo, Geri and several members of her group stood near the rear of the Pegasus rechecking their equipment.

"You really think what's down there was built by aliens," one of the USGS scientists asked Dr. Geraldo.

"I'm not sure. But, we'll know more information when we get there."

Captain Bonar's voice boomed through the intercom.

"Lieutenant-Commander Tarkenston, you have a green launch."

"Yes sir. Okay, everyone take a seat and strap in. We're cleared to disembark. STANCE, initiate launch sequence and deploy Pegasus."

"Pegasus away, Captain," the operations officer announced.

"LC, go in on manual. Give the Cerberus time to survey the area and to find an entry point. The other team ran into strong deep water currents, so set your stabilizers to seventy-five percent maximum."

"Aye—aye sir, roger that. Switching to manual, setting stabilizers at point seven five."

A third of the way down, Professor Rosenbaum noticed something out the starboard portal. She leaned nearer to the glass.

"What is that?" she whispered.

Doctor Stolte overheard her.

"What is what?" he asked.

She pointed out a portal.

"That—! What are those lights—? See them?"

"Yes—I do. Lieutenant-Commander we've got company off the starboard bow."

The LC gazed out of a nearby portal.

"STANCE, initiate AP."

"Auto pilot engaged."

"Captain, we've got bogeys. I got nothing on AI or standard radar—visual only. Objects do not, I repeat, do not appear hostile."

"Copy that, Lieutenant-Commander. Proceed with caution and do not take evasive action unless entities appear aggressive," replied Captain Bonar.

"Copy that."

"I take it this was expected?" Geri asked.

"Intel said it was probable. There's been a lot of activity in this area the last couple of weeks," said the LC.

The team stared out the forward hemispherical dome and portals at the bright lights. There were five in total. The largest of the objects progressed parallel to the Pegasus, glowing white. Smaller ones glowed yellow and darted around the submersible like hummingbirds. They moved about through water with ease. There were no obvious sources of propulsion or any noticeable water displacement emanating from the USOs.

"Lieutenant-Commander Tarkenston, what's your status?" radioed the Captain.

"We still have multiple bogies, sir."

"Any changes in their behavior?"

"Objects appear curious only, sir. No aggressive tendencies," said the Lieutenant.

"Captain, I got an energy spike emanating five meters off the Pegasus port bow," the Comtac officer reported. "It seems to be low intensity."

"LC, we're reading low energy bursts from your port."

"I have it localized, sir. AI identified it with a ninety-seven percent probability as a low intensity scanning wave."

"Good, stay on course and let them look as long as they want."

"Lieutenant Mitchell, have you located a way in?" Captain Bonar asked.

"Approaching Z point now, sir," she responded.

"Acknowledged—deploy CPB rotating frequencies."

In nineteen thirty-seven, Nikola Tesla announced to reporters at a press conference that he was on the verge of discovering an entirely new source of energy. Frustrated in his attempts to generate interest and financing for his peace beam, he sent an elaborate technical paper, including diagrams, to a number of Allied nations, including the United States, Canada, England, France, the Soviet Union, and Yugoslavia. Tesla's idea, though publicly never taken seriously, was secretly researched by the Department of Defense.

"STANCE, deploy forward particle beam," said Lieutenant Mitchell.

From an opening in the bow of the Cerberus arose an oddly-shaped projector.

"Particle beam deployed and ready, Lieutenant Mitchell," replied the AI.

"Captain, CPB shows fully charged. We are ready to fire."

"Initiate firing sequence, lieutenant—thirty-five percent OP—fire when ready."

"Roger that. Firing particle beam, sir."

A narrow blue shaft of light emanated from the projector. It struck the wall of the structure and then expanded in a circular shape. Moments later, Lieutenant Mitchell contacted the Argo.

"No change from the structure, sir, and I'm reading a malfunction on the aft thruster intake valves."

Captain Bonar looked at the video feed.

"We see it, Mitch," he responded.

"Lieutenant, is the pulsed acceleration data showing yellow?" Dr. Nashikato asked.

"Yes sir."

"There's a problem with the positive to negative ion transition. Bring her back topside on manual after deployment."

"Mitch, rotate frequencies and go to fifty-five percent OP," said the captain.

"Yes sir."

Access to the structure was immediate, as part of the wall began to retract, confirming a hidden entrance.

"We have access," Lieutenant Mitchell reported.

Captain Bonar studied the opening via video carefully.

"Proceed with caution, Mitch," he responded.

At point five throughsters only, the Cerberus eased forward. When it reached the entrance, several rays of light emanating from inside, surrounded the submersible. It immediately rendered the controls nonfunctional.

"Captain, we have a problem. The energy beam has disabled helm control and is pulling us into the structure. Maneuvering throughsters are offline."

The captain picked up a dossier and radioed back the submersible.

"Go with it, Lieutenant. Intel has it on the chart."

"Yes sir," she replied, her heart returning to normal rhythm.

The beam consumed the Cerberus, pulling it past the threshold where an unseen force held the water back from flooding inside the edifice. It maneuvered the craft upon a docking platform and sat it down with a slight thud. Partial power inside the structure activated, illuminating the area. The Cerberus regained full functionality.

"STANCE, run full diagnostic and give me a channel to the Argo," Lieutenant Mitchell requested.

"Captain, Zebra A point accomplished, Cerberus secure."

"Roger that, Lieutenant. We're reading breathable air, no contaminants. You have a go for disembark."

Lieutenant Mitchell used the internal Com to relay the message to the Special Ops Team.

"Sergeant, Captain Bonar reports we have a go."

"Okay, ladies, keep it simple and by the book," the sergeant reminded his men.

Lieutenant Mitchell entered a code on a keypad near the Cerberus navigation joystick. The starboard hatch unlocked, then unfolded. Another hatch near the pilot's seat also decompressed, and then opened. The soldiers abandoned the

Cerberus one by one, arms to the ready. Using hand signals, they set up an immediate perimeter. Roughly about ten square acres, the site was enormous.

Sergeant Davidson turned to Lieutenant Mitchell who squatted next to him besides the stern of the submersible.

"This must be a hangar bay," he said.

Platforms identical to one that supported the Cerberus lined the wall. The structure was empty of any recognizable ships or other vehicles. Besides several consoles with no buttons, knobs or other distinguishable features, the hangar bay contained very little technology. With another set of hand signals, Sergeant Davidson ordered his men to expand the perimeter. After securing the area, Davidson reported in.

"Black Jackal to Foxhole, Black Jackal to Foxhole, over."

"This is Captain Bonar Sergeant. What ya got?"

"Sir, the immediate area is secure, no activity."

"Good."

The captain turned to the communications operator.

"Notify the Pegasus to proceed."

"Yes sir," he acknowledged.

Captain Bonar continued his exchange with Davidson.

"Sergeant . . . Pegasus in route . . . ETA five minutes. Do not leave the immediate area until she arrives, then send the Cerberus back topside."

"Copy that—out," Sergeant Davidson responded.

He gathered his men.

Guarding the entrance, TJ and Danny Boy stood eagerly awaiting orders. They were the youngest of the team and had grown up together in the Dissected Till Plains of Nebraska. A region of gently rolling hills, eighty-nine percent of the cities in the state had fewer than 3,000 people and hundreds had fewer than 1,000. The boys grew up in one of those small towns and were childhood friends. TJ's father and Danny Boy's father were the best of friends, and so were their grandfathers and their grandfathers before them. All had been military men. The "Boys", as they were fondly called, had join the United States Marine Corps together and were assigned to the Maritime Special Purpose Force.

The New World Order fragmented across economic, political, religious and ethnic lines producing global instability characterized by a wide diversity and dispersion of potential threats to U.S. interests. Since the inception of the Marine Expeditionary Unit Special Operations Capable, the likelihood of executing precision direct action missions increased dramatically. The Maritime Special Purpose Force gave commanders low profile surgical capability.

TJ and Danny Boy were the best of the best. They were the generation Y soldiers. A Dutch newspaper once referred to Generation Y as the Einstein Generation, referring to the ability to perform many activities at the same time. They were the first to grow up immersed in a digital and internet driven world. While older soldiers struggled with the new technology sweeping through the military, it was second nature to "The Boys". When under fire, it was as if the two were playing a video game. They were exceptional soldiers individually, but together they were superb.

"ETA Pegasus, five minutes. Look sharp, gentlemen," barked Sergeant Davidson. "TJ, Danny Boy, stay on the door. After the submersible comes through, nothing or nobody else gets in. Got it?"

"Got it, El Capitan," said Danny Boy.

TJ slapped the back of his head.

"Come on, boys—focus. Harris, you and Dickerson set up over there and there," Sergeant Davidson pointed. "Lieutenant Mitchell, get the Cerberus prepped for departure just in case. Tank, you're with me."

Tank removed a portable missile launcher from the Cerberus. If anything besides the Pegasus came across the entrance threshold, it would pay . . . and pay dearly.

Following the encounter with the unidentified objects, the second submersible arrived a few minutes later. Just as the Cerberus, the structure's systems remotely guided the Pegasus inside, and then sat the submersible on a docking platform. After running a full diagnostic on the underwater craft, Lieutenant-Commander Tarkenston and the scientists disembarked.

"Glad you could join us," Sergeant Davidson greeted Geri. It's a pretty big place. It'll take hours to explore the entire area. First, we have to get the Cerberus back in the water. Got any ideas?"

Geri slowly scanned the area from ceiling to floor.

"Have you seen anything resembling a control panel?"

"There are several consoles over here with a couple of symbols on them."

They walked toward the front of the Cerberus. The console sat on a pedestal about four feet in height. Geri walked around it, studying it carefully. She removed her backpack and pulled a PDA from the side pocket. Accessing some information on the device, she touched the symbols on the side of the pedestal. It was obvious she knew exactly what to look for and what to do when she found it. Sergeant Davidson looked on as Geri accessed the structures systems. The remaining consoles activated simultaneously, lighting up the entire structure.

"There, that should do it," she said nonchalantly. "Lieutenant Mitchell, get aboard the Cerberus and prepare for departure."

"Yes ma'am."

Geri went to a different console, then another. Accessing the system on the third and in an exacting order, she pushed another set of anomalous cryptograms. The Cerberus quietly lifted off the docking pad. Assisted by an unseen force, it glided toward the aperture then back into the abyss. After radioing the Argo, the submersible headed back topside.

"Nice going, Doc," complimented Sergeant Davidson as the Cerberus went through the threshold.

Geri removed a multifunctional GPS device from her backpack and glanced at the display.

"We're headed this way," she pointed with the gadget.

"I think we should stick together on account of this place being the size that it is," Davidson replied. "TJ, Danny Boy, on point."

Harris, Tank and Dickerson brought up the rear.

After several meters, the team came upon a large room filled with statues, old coins, artifacts and other antiquities. Mendel Hanrahan took pictures.

"What is this place?" Lieutenant-Commander Tarkenston asked.

"It's a storage room. From the looks of it, the stuff is from all different cultures and eras," Professor Harry Tanaka answered.

He ran his fingers through a bowl of coins sitting atop a pedestal. Doctor Hanrahan took more pictures of gold and silver coins.

"But, how can this be?"

Oxford educated, Professor Rosenbaum, slowly walked around a pristine sarcophagus admiring its immaculate hieroglyphs.

"A man once said—'The hypotheses we accept ought to explain phenomena which we have observed.' However, they ought to do more than this: our hypotheses ought to foretell phenomena which have not yet been observed—hence, what is—what must be."

"What does that mean?" Lieutenant-Commander Tarkenston asked.

"It means these artifacts from all over the world, from different centuries, are here—right here right now. So expect more surprises," said Geri.

"We'll come back and take an inventory later. Right now we need to keep moving."

The scientist left the room reluctantly. According to Professor Tanaka, there were probably at least several hundred separate chambers of different shapes and sizes in the structure. Thus far, some held artifacts while others contained large groups of consoles. As they penetrated deeper into the edifice, the team discovered an unusual room. It would have gone unnoticed had Dickerson not detected a temperature difference.

Removing a flashlight from his vest, he went in to explore it.

"Hey, take a look at this."

The team followed him into the dimly lit room. Geri searched for a control console. The room was much larger than the previously explored and indeed, noticeably cooler.

Tank noticed light reflecting off an object near an alcove. Followed by Dr. Stolte, Professor Tanaka, and Dr. Hanrahan, he went to investigate. As they reached the source, the enormous room brightened.

"There, that should do it," said Geri as she released a pad on a small console.

Along the walls and entrenched into the floor, the chamber was filled with individual translucent pods. Condensation settled on the glass, making it difficult to see inside. Doctor Hanrahan approached the nearest pod and wiped it with his hand. He stared for a moment, unwilling to believe his eyes. Shaken, he stumbled backwards, bumping into TJ. Unable to speak, he pointed.

"What is it, Doc? What did you see?" Danny Boy asked, approaching the glass casing.

He put his face against it and peered through.

"Geez . . . it's Godzilla."

TJ pulled him away.

"Get outta here. What you looking at?" he asked.

His mouth froze open.

Professor Tanaka and Dr. Stolte pushed forward to see for themselves. Peering back through the glass, dead or in suspended animation, was a creature that hadn't walked the earth in eons. Bipedaled, the animal was about eight feet long and stood five feet at the shoulders. Its serrated teeth glistened from the glow of Dickerson's flashlight. Dark cold eyes stared, their emptiness apparent. In what seemed like a last desperate attempt at freedom, its claws lay frozen, clutching against the frigid sterile glass.

"These must be cryonics chambers," said Geri.

"What'd she say?" asked Danny Boy.

"Stasis pods... yeah, but what's inside of them?' Sergeant Davidson asked.

"Well, my paleontology is a little rusty, but I believe this is a Juravenator," Doctor Hanrahan answered. "It's an animal that walked the earth around one hundred fifty million years ago."

"Hey, you hear that, TJ? We found the terminator," Danny Boy joked. "Who would have thunk it."

After looking into the eyes of the frozen reptile, TJ was already in threat mode.

"Shut up, dude. This is serious," he snapped.

"There must be hundreds of these things in here. Maybe even thousands," said Lieutenant-Commander Tarkenston.

Dr. Stolte moved several chambers down and wiped the condensation from the glass.

"Come over here and take a look at this."

He snapped several pictures as the team gathered around him.

"What's in this... what is that?... a monkey?" Harris asked.

"That's Australopithecus. Australopithecus Africanus to be exact... an ancestor of Homo sapiens. They inhabited the earth roughly three million years ago," answered Professor Tanaka.

Professor Rosenbaum pulled Geri aside.

"I know this is going to sound crazy, but I think what we have here is alien technology that's able to transport animate and inanimate objects through time. I mean, how else can you explain it?"

"That doesn't sound crazy at all," replied Geri. "We still have a lot of ground to cover, so let's move on."

After many more photos, they left the room through a connecting corridor.

It led to another chamber filled with star charts of galaxies and other astronomical objects. Activated earlier by Geri in the main bay, they projected in a three-dimensional form, above four groupings of eight consoles. Professor Rosenbaum recognized them immediately.

"Take a look at this," she pointed. "It's our galaxy, the Milky Way, Canis Major Dwarf galaxy and I believe . . . this one is the Large Magellanic Cloud if I'm not mistaken."

"This is incredible," said Dr. Stolte as he took more pictures.

Huddled around one of the larger pedestals, the team observed spiral and elliptical galaxies, black holes and other interstellar phenomena. Unable to access the control panel on the console, the team continued. Geri glanced at her handheld device, and then approached a long corridor. Scrutinized by a green, low energy shaft of light, she pressed on. Cryogenic chambers occupied both sides of the walkway. The LC stopped and stared at one of the inhabitants. Behind the glass and perfectly preserved, a faint light revealed an extremely beautiful woman wearing a tall headdress and ornate jewelry made of gold and colorful beads. She wore a linen dress that hung over the shoulders with straps.

"Queen Nefertiti. She was chief royal wife of Pharaoh Akhenaten of ancient Egypt's New Kingdom. She vanished from the historical record after the 14th year of Akhenaten's 17-year reign. Now we know why," said Professor Tanaka.

He continued to the next chamber.

"Henry Hudson . . . disappeared in 1694 after a mutiny by his crew during the exploration of the Hudson Bay region. Felix Moncla disappeared while hunting an unidentified flying object over the U.S.-Canadian border. Donald Crowhurst, an English businessman and amateur sailor, went missing in 1970 while competing in a single-handed round the world yacht race."

"These are people that have been abducted?" the LC asked.

"It would appear so," Dr. Hanrahan replied.

"Keep moving, gentleman," said Sergeant Davidson.

Geri placed her device next to a panel and pressed several keys. The doorway opened.

"This is it," said Geri.

She returned the device back to its pocket.

Near the middle of the room lay a group of pedestals, eight in the outer circle and four in an inner circle. In the middle of the four large pedestals stood a platform with symbols located on the top and sides. A large crystal in the shape of a square antiprism, sat on top of a pedestal on a large platform. Geri investigated each console starting with the outer group. She then approached the pedestal followed by the team. As they stood on the platform, the crystal began to glow. The team watched as its brilliance intensified, changing its shape. The room then went dark.

Chapter Eleven
Medan, Sumatra

Medan was a mix of communities, reflecting its pre- and post-independence history. It was Indonesia's third most populous after Jakarta and Surabaya, with approximately 2.5 million people.

The cab ride from Polonia International Airport to the Inna Dharma Deli Medan was only supposed to be a fifteen-minute drive, but because of the traffic and other inconveniences of a large city, it took a almost a hour.

David studied the scenery while the taxi driver blew the horn and screamed at pedestrians and other motorists. They went past a park with children playing soccer. It brought back memories of his childhood.

He could only recall a few good things about those years. The permeating aroma of apples and oranges hidden away in a dark closet by his mother until Christmas, and the championship baseball game when he was heroically lifted up on his team's shoulders, to name a few.

Sports were one of very few means of escape from the instability at home, and mostly everyone participated in athletic competition in the neighborhood and at school. David played baseball and basketball and like his siblings, was an exceptional athlete. When he wasn't in his mother's kitchen trying to create the cure for some exotic disease or buried in science books, he shagged flies or played tag football in vacant lots filled with rubble and waste.

Through schoolbooks, he explored other worlds far away from the smothering darkness that consumed his. Although he enjoyed any literature on natural sciences, books on astronomy, physics or paleontology were his favorites. David imagined himself visiting one of Saturn's moons. Wearing his modified spacesuit, he'd discover microscopic life forms that held genetics secrets for curing all diseases and world hunger. He hungered for a deeper understanding of the universe—of life. Sometimes after pushing his mind to its comprehendible limits, he stood on the edge of a chasm, unable to access the other side. To David, his quest for perceptiveness felt almost spiritual.

He took a long breath and sat back in his seat. His thoughts were now of Geri and how special she was to him. He gave in to her, awakening something precious and long forgotten deep inside him. She started his journey of trust and confidence. When traumatized, the human spirit of the innocent manifests itself as a dark cloud of distrust and emotional seclusion. Fear slowly eats away at the soul, consuming character, strength and will. When one has experienced it for so long, it becomes comfortable like old leather. David's past nearly eroded his will until Geri nurtured the last remaining seeds of his soul. Sometimes, all you need is someone to believe in you. She did.

#

The taxi pulled up to the hotel. The Inna Dharma Deli was located in the heart of Medan. It offered conveniently equipped rooms with an air-conditioning system, cold and hot water, video programs, piped music, telephones, and international TV programs through a parabolic antenna system. It also had various hotel facilities like swimming pools, restaurants and conference rooms. The best choice to stay for visitors in the region, it was conveniently a short distance from modern shopping centers, banks, government offices, private companies, the post office, railway station, and other public facilities. The driver removed a large suitcase and carried it into the hotel. Dr. Woodall followed with smaller hand baggage. He paid the driver and tipped him generously after reaching the check-in counter.

"Dr. David Woodall checking in," he informed the clerk.

The woman handed him a key card.

"Yes sir. Here is your key, sir. Room one seventy-eight. Is there anything else, sir?" asked the clerk.

"Has Sharon or Rutherford Geraldo checked in?"

Typing on a keyboard, the clerk searched the hotel registry.

"Yes sir, Mr. Geraldo has checked in. However, Mrs. Geraldo has not arrived yet."

"They're not married; they're father and daughter," said David.

"Oh. Excuse me, sir. Yes, Mr. Geraldo is in room one seventy-four and Mrs. Geraldo has not check in yet."

Noticeably weary from the journey, David's next response was blunt.

"You said that already. What room do you have listed for her?"

The clerk searched the records again.

"Room one seventy-six, sir."

David took a long breath and reached for the handle of the suitcase. He focused on the clerk's nametag.

"Please except my apologies . . . Sujatmi. I'm a little tired from the trip. Excuse me for my impoliteness."

"Yes sir. Okay. Thank you, sir," said the clerk, bowing.

He removed the other bag from the counter and headed down the hallway, reaching his room just in time to see Admiral Rutherford Geraldo opening his door.

"David, how have you been? Good to see you again," said the surprised admiral.

They shook hands.

"Geri didn't tell me you were coming."

"It's good to see you, too, sir. It was kind of a last-minute decision. She called the other day and told me to meet both of you here at the hotel."

"She isn't here. David, do you still have level three security clearance?" Admiral Geraldo asked.

"Yes sir, I do. Is she in some type of trouble? What was she working on?"

Admiral Geraldo looked down the hall, first to the left then to the right.

"Come on in and I'll explain," he said.

Carrying a travel case and pulling his luggage, Dr. Woodall entered the admiral's room.

"Have a seat, David. Would you like a drink?"

"No thank you, sir. Where is Geri?"

"My daughter was working on a black ops project, code name Inside Awake. In October of nineteen ninety-eight, a National Reconnaissance Office top-secret satellite located a structure deep in the Sunda Trench. Two weeks ago, the NRO satellite picked up a transmission emanating from inside the structure. A team of scientists along with military support personnel, was assembled and dispatched to investigate. They've been out of contact for about five hours now."

"And Geri, she was a member of the civilian team? She never mentioned it," said David.

"I know how close you two are. She pleaded with me to go. I made her promise that if I could get her in, she wouldn't discuss it with anyone—-not even with you. After the satellite picked up the signal, we had multiple reports of unidentified flying objects and other strange incidents occurring from Africa to Antarctica."

"Antarctica?"

"Yes, even Antarctica," said the admiral.

He removed a number of photographs from a briefcase and handed them to David.

"A U.S. Geological Survey team found a crop circle, or I guess you would call it an ice circle, near the South Pole. Several people died in Tanzania when an object came out of a nearby lake, then roasted nearly an entire village."

David flipped through the photos carefully. He noticed several pictograms.

"Wait a minute, I've seen this. I've seen these symbols before," he said.

He pointed at the aerial picture of the ice circle.

"What? Where?"

"On a metallic like box that was found somewhere in South America," replied David. "It's on an artifact I've been researching in Zurich."

In the middle of the circle was an exact replica of the object.

"I have a bad feeling about this," David said nervously. "While I was doing experiments on the relic, I noticed it changed shape and it emitted unidentifiable energy waves that could have been theoretical particles of Tachyon. I have a theory on what the box might be. If I'm right, Geri and the others are in danger."

"Danger? W—hat sort of danger?"

"The eight symbols on the box represent a new order, the beginning of a new era. Eight represents regeneration and resurrection. The four symbols is the number of all things that have a beginning, all things made of material things, even matter itself. The four cardinal directions: east, west, north and south; the four seasons: spring, winter, fall and summer; the four dimensions: length, width, height and time. Time is the key. Somehow, the object is able to manipulate temporal time by changing the fundamental frequency in the universe, which is about 1.855×1043 Hz. I think we're dealing with beings that have developed technology not only to visit our world, but also to visit our history. And if the structure is related to the box and the ice circle, and I'm sure it is—Geri and your people may not be in our time anymore."

David paced back and forth in front of the bed.

"Admiral Geraldo, you said that a satellite picked up a transmission. Were your people able to determine an energy signature?" he asked.

"Through analysis, they determined it emitted ultra-high-energy subatomic particles along a narrow beam toward an empty region of space. When we lost communication with the team, the signal stopped transmitting."

"Let's assume the technology is used as a time portal by creating a closed time-like curve."

"What are you getting at?" asked Admiral Geraldo.

"Try to imagine time as a series of events along a line. By focusing enough energy, theoretically, you can bend that line to visit the past. Once you're in the past, you'd need a device to return. Think of it as an electrical circuit, a closed loop. I think the device was somehow activated and took them somewhere in the past where another mechanism is located to bring them back."

"So, you believe one end of the connection is in this lab and the other is with the team?"

"Exactly. I have to get back there. The artifact is a hyper-dimensional device of some sort. They found it next to dinosaur bones. If I am right, someone or something went back to the Mesozoic Era and lost it. I just hope it's programmed to get back to the original time coordinates."

"I've already sent a couple of copters to the ship's location. They should be contacting me within the next hour or so. You get back to that lab and figure out a way to activate that thing or we'll never see any of them again," said Admiral Geraldo. "I'm going to make some calls."

Dr. Woodall went to his room. He hurriedly unpacked a few things and picked up the phone.

"Hotel Operator," acknowledged a voice from the earpiece.

"Yes, can you dial Switzerland 044-826-74-11 please?"

There was a long pause and then a voice spoke on the other end.

"Europélaboratorium för partikelfysikkomplex Schweitz. Hur kan jag hjälpa dig?"

"Dr. William Jamison, please."

"Your security code, sir?" the operator asked.

"Tango Beta Tango Alpha six eight Tango Beta."

"Thank you, Dr. Woodall. Dr. Jamison is currently unavailable."

"I'd like to leave a message for him. Tell him I'll be back sooner than expected . . . tomorrow."

"Thank you, Doctor Woodall. I will relay your message."

As David hung up the phone, a knock at the door interrupted his thoughts. Not waiting for the door to open fully, Admiral Geraldo forced himself inside.

"I just got word from the Argo. She was in Dead Star mode and unable to transmit long range. The commanding officer said the members wore tracking devices that monitored their position and they've lost contact with the team. They sent a backup team down and they couldn't locate them. It's as if they just vanished into thin air."

David slowly slumped on the edge of the bed.

"Okay, that's it then. I'm going back to the lab. The artifact is one of the few clues we have."

"David, if you need any help or anything—let me know. I'm going to get more people out there to see if they can find any answers."

Dr. Woodall repacked his belongings and took the first flight to Zurich.

Chapter Twelve
Saltopus

The military team immediately drew their weapons to the ready position as the darkness surrounding the group gradually lifted.

"What the hell just happened? A second ago we were looking at a bright light in a room four miles beneath the ocean," said Dickerson.

"I don't know. Harris, what's our position?"

"Something tells me we're not in Kansas anymore," Danny Boy whispered nervously.

Harris removed a GPS device from his pocket.

"I got nothin', Sergeant. I got nothin'."

"What do you mean nothing, soldier?"

"No signal, sir. I got no signal."

"It must be malfunctioning. Dickerson, Tank, check yours."

"He's right, sir. Nothing overhead to triangulate with," said Tank.

"Same here," said Dickerson. "I can't get a signal either."

"Check for interference."

A large thunderous sound reverberated through the forest. Sergeant Davidson held up a closed fist prompting everyone to become silent and stationary. With hand signals only, he motioned his men to take up defensive positions fifteen yards out on the perimeter—two men forward at the eleven and one o'clock, two men rear at the four and seven o'clock, and one man at the nine o'clock position. The sergeant then attempted to contact the Argo. He activated his tactical headset, then adjusted his microphone to whisper mode.

"Black jackal to foxhole, over; black jackal to foxhole, over; do you read, foxhole? Foxhole, this is black jackal, over."

He checked the transmitter.

"Radio check, radio check, over."

His team responded. Trying to sound confident, he addressed the civilian scientist.

"There must be some type of interference with the radio signal that's keeping us from transmitting long range. Anybody care to take a good swag at where we are?"

"What's swag?" asked Dr. Stolte.

"A scientific wild ass guess. Anybody want to give it a shot?"

No one responded. Dr. Stolte walked over to a small group of plants and carefully examined their leaves and stalk. His eyes widen as he hurriedly moved to another cluster nearby.

"This is unbelievable," he exclaimed.

The other scientists huddled around him as he held a leaf, examining the back and front.

"What is it? What's so fascinating about a leaf?" Professor Rosenbaum asked.

"Nothing really, except this Glossopteris. It's been extinct for about two hundred million years," Dr. Stolte responded.

"Let me see that."

The scientist handed the plant to Geri.

"Are you sure about this, John?" she asked, examining it.

"Great, Jurassic Park all over again," said Danny Boy.

"No, not exactly Jurassic," responded Dr. Stolte as he slowly walked over to another small tree-like plant.

He touched its foliage, inspecting it carefully.

"This flora—Dicroidium—it's of the Triassic period."

He noticed something hiding behind nearby ferns. Slowly reaching down then moving his hand quickly, he seized and lifted a green yellowish animal. About the size of a small cat, it was roughly two feet long, weighed about two pounds, and had two hands, each with five fingers. The animal struggled to escape. Its long head with lots of very sharp teeth and razor-like claws made it difficult for the scientist to control. Dr. Stolte held up his trophy by the tail.

"And this, my fellow time travelers—is a Saltopus of the late Triassic period."

Geri let out a deep sigh and sat down on a fallen tree.

"Good heavens. Somehow we've been transported back in time two hundred, twenty million years.

"Holy shit ... Danny Boy, TJ, Dickerson, Harris, Tank, get back here now," Sergeant Davidson ordered over his radio.

The men quickly assembled together with the civilian team in the small clearing. The Saltopus continued to struggle to free itself from Dr. Stolte's firm grip. Utterly agitated, it suddenly shrieked loudly.

"John, the animal is going to attract other predators. I suggest you release it," said Geri.

Dr. Stolte freed the shrieking biped behind a large fern as more of the creatures ran through the underbrush.

"I agree. Who knows what we may face while were here. Does anybody have an idea how we can get back?" asked Sergeant Davidson.

"The good news is the Triassic is the pre-dinosaur period. They're just starting to evolve," Dr. Hanrahan said.

"Good, that means we have nothing to worry about, right? T-Rex won't be chasing us like in the movies, right?" Danny Boy asked nervously.

"Don't get me wrong, soldier. The Triassic had its fair share of carnivores. Some small, like the animal we just observed, and some large, very large. As far as getting back, well, that's another story altogether."

"My guess is something was activated while we were standing on the platform. Maybe a wormhole generator," Professor Rosenbaum added.

"Does anybody remember touching anything?" Geri asked.

"Nothing was touched and no one went close to any of the consoles. Maybe the platform was the catalyst," said Doctor Hanrahan.

"I thought time travel was impossible," said Lieutenant-Commander Tarkenston.

"There's several theories regarding time travel. For instance a wormhole, if harnessed and portable, might allow us to travel to the past as well as the future," Professor Rosenbaum continued. "There's also a theory regarding Cosmic Strings."

"This is all fascinating stuff, but my priority is to get everyone safely back to the Argo," Sergeant Davidson interrupted.

"Hopefully, the creators of the technology also built a way home," said Geri. "It's just a matter of locating it, then figuring out how it works."

"I suggest we find shelter first. Although the dinosaurs haven't fully evolved and most of them are relatively still small, there are plenty of dangerous animals around."

Dr. Hanrahan looked at Danny Boy.

"And yes, soldier, just like the movie, there's raptors—Eoraptors. It's a fierce hunter, a meat eater, smart and fast. Its teeth are serrated, but the animal is only about a foot high and about three feet long, so I wouldn't worry if I was you."

Hoping to find refuge in a cave or possibly another structure, they decided to explore the immediate area first.

The Triassic was a time of transition. It followed the largest extinction event in the history of life, and so it was a time when the survivors of that event spread and re-colonized. The formation of the super continent of Pangaea at the beginning of the Triassic decreased the amount of shoreline, formed mountains, altering global climate and ocean circulation. The climate was generally hot and dry, with strong seasonality that included both arid dune environments and moist river and lake habitats. Seed ferns like Glossopteris and early species of gymnosperms dominated the terrain. While a large volcano was noticeable through Sergeant Davidson's binoculars roughly one hundred miles away, the surrounding area consisted of ferns and Cycads with tufts of tough, palm-like leaves and a woody trunk.

Hoping to find water, they headed toward an area with thicker undergrowth. They also hoped the vegetation would thwart an ambush from larger predators.

A U.S. Navy special warfare unit Beach Jumper, Tank took point as the group trudged through the prehistoric forest. A muscular, six foot four specimen and the oldest member of the Special Ops Team, he was in superb physical condition. Beach Jumpers had a mysterious power to cloud men's minds, though it came from the study and development of tactics rather than traveling in the Orient. Recruited for prolonged, hazardous, distant duty for secret projects, their identities and activities were very highly classified. The slightest leak of information could ruin even brilliant deceptions. Many went to their graves without ever revealing, even to their wives and children, what they had done in the Navy. Tank was old school. He didn't joke much, he didn't talk much, but he got the job done.

Dickerson, a Special Forces Operational Detachment-Delta soldier, commonly referred to as Delta Force by the public, headed up the rear. He had the highest aptitude rating of any team member. Although extremely versatile and fully capable of taking on any number of mission profiles, his primary tasks involved counter-terrorism. "Dick", as his fellow soldiers sometimes jokingly referred to him, was a man of extreme details. Carrying his M4 5.56 mm Carbine, he followed behind the group, cautiously listening between each footstep.

They neared a small glade. Lieutenant-Commander Tarkenston swatted at bothersome insects.

"I think they like you," TJ joked.

"I certainly didn't join the Navy for this," said the LC.

A primitive cricket with six-inch wings landed on his shoulder.

"Get it off, get it off," he yelled.

"What the hell are you trying to do, give away our position? Keep your damn mouth shut," Sergeant Davidson whispered sternly.

He removed the beetle with his hands and placed it on the ground.

"It'll be getting dark soon. We'll make camp here. Danny Boy, TJ, gather some wood," Sergeant Davidson ordered.

He knelt on one knee, grabbed a stick and drew in the dirt.

"I want a ring of small fires around point A here."

He jabbed a hole in the soil with a circle around it.

"Harris, Dickerson, thirty yards from the perimeter of the fires, I want Claymores with trip wires, here, here, here, and here. Tank—forty yards out, set up barbed spike plates—plenty of them. I want to hear what's coming before it gets here."

The Triassic was a dangerous time and place for any animal, but at night, it was treacherous. The first mammals appeared in the late Triassic. They were small, roughly about the size of mice and nocturnal. As time passed, predators evolved to hunt the primitive, warm-blooded nocturnal vertebrates. Later, bigger and deadlier carnivores evolved to hunt the hunters.

It was a long and restless night for everyone. The fires kept most of the bigger reptiles away from the encampment. Occasionally, a mine would explode from a creature hitting a trip wire, causing debris to fall on nearby vegetation. Frightening death cries resonated across the valley as six-foot long wooden spikes impaled creatures throughout the night. TJ and Danny Boy spent most of their time wagering on how long it would take before the next victim met its demise, and from which direction it would originate. It was indeed a long night, especially for the civilians.

Being of Japanese heritage and a man of honor, before dawn, Professor Tanaka insisted on going into the forest to defecate. Dickerson had given him a MRE earlier and he had greedily eaten it. Unable to sleep, he arose from his hard patch of soil and approached Harris who was on watch.

"I would like to use the bathroom."

"Sorry Doc, but the restrooms are closed for cleaning until morning," Harris replied.

He looked at the scientist, amused.

"You'll have to use the bathrooms inside the perimeter, Doc. It's not safe out there. If you don't get blown up or run through with a stake, something with teeth is going to tear you apart."

Professor Tanaka became agitated. He clutched his stomach in distress.

"There's no way in hell I'm going to pull down my pants in front of these people. I am an honorable man and I demand to be escorted so I can relieve myself," he said vehemently.

Harris, who had been sitting on a tree stump, stood up. Six feet six, he definitely fit the Seal Creed.

In times of war or uncertainty, there's a special breed of warrior ready to answer the nation's call; a common man with uncommon desire to succeed. Forged by adversity, he stands alongside America's finest special operations forces to serve his country, the American people, and protect their way of life. Harris was that man. He'd performed heroically in Desert Shield and Desert Storm, and most recently in Operation Enduring Freedom in Afghanistan. Furthermore, he'd served on all continents and under all conditions. However, he did have his limits when it came to civilians.

"Doc, there's a spot right behind this stump. I'll stand in front of you so no one can see," he said plainly.

This only displeased the scientist further.

"How dare you, you son of a . . ."

"Now wait a minute, Professor," Sergeant Davidson interrupted. "I'm not going to risk the lives of my men so you can go into the woods to take a crap—and keep your damn voice down."

Stunned, Professor Tanaka marched back to join the others. He lay on the ground apart from the group until he was certain no one was attentive. After borrowing a small flashlight from Geri while she slept, he crept away into the darkness.

The professor headed toward the thickest part of the forest to conceal any evidence of his presence and to avoid mines or booby traps. The night was alive with primeval sounds. A cool gentle wind blew across the valley, a welcomed relief from the dreadful heat experienced earlier during the day. After finding a suitable place, he placed the flashlight in his mouth and pulled down his pants. As he crouched, he hoped his flatulence wouldn't attract any unwanted attention. He brushed away a stubborn leaf. A primitive mammal raced across his foot chasing a beetle, followed by a small reptile. The professor briefly stood up, shook his foot, and then continued his business. A sudden gust blew through the flora carrying with it the smell of decaying flesh. He trusted the source of the aroma was far away. As Professor Tanaka turned to brush the leaf away again, he felt a sharp pain emanating from his groin. Terrifying thoughts quickly raced through his mind.

"Teeth . . . no God, please, please don't let it be teeth."

He stood up quickly, leaping off the ground. A small Saltopus hung on for dear life. Professor Tanaka stumbled backwards, the flashlight still firmly between his teeth. He seized the animal's neck, struggling to remove its sharp incisors. With his pants around his ankles, he tripped, got up, and hastily shuffled deeper into the forest. The reptile's body swung violently as other juvenile Saltopus gave chase. The professor fell, inadvertently activating one of Tank's booby traps. Long sharp spears barely missed as they whizzed past his head. Several penetrated the soft skin of a fern tree. The professor raised his eyes, dropping the flashlight from his mouth. The sight of a spear impaled into the primitive plant causes him to panic further. The other Saltopus saw their opening. He unleashed a chilling cry as the group attacked him viciously. The reverberation of exploding claymores muffled the scientist's pleas. They went unanswered.

The sun finally rose, bringing a new sense of optimism to the expedition. Geri and Sergeant Davidson discussed their options.

"What does the field manual say about situations like this? Probably find the nearest tree and climb as high as possible."

"Not exactly, but we'll have to find water and shelter as quickly as possible. My men are rationing what little they have left in the canteens. It won't last very long."

"The temperature must be around one hundred twenty degrees during the day and not much cooler at night. Keep an eye out for symptoms of heat stroke."

"We'll try to keep everyone cool by resting in the shade as often as we can, but the sooner we get out of this sun the better."

"Try to stick to the underbrush as much as possible. When the animals give birth, the offspring will run there so they won't be eaten. If it's the safest place for them, it's the safest for us."

"That's pretty much what the manual says—whatever the objective was before—now it's about survival."

"Yeah, that's true, but your men are trained for it—we're not."

"That's the funny thing about the human spirit, Doc—the will to survive is built in. Keep an eye on your people and don't let them wander off alone. I have a feeling some of them may see this place as a playground—someplace to explore."

"I'll remind them to stay together."

Dr. Hanrahan was the first to notice Professor Tanaka's absence. He half-heartedly called out for him in order not to attract any unwanted attention. The other scientists joined him as he sauntered back and forth, his eyes trying to pierce the dense underbrush.

"Where is Professor Tanaka?" Geri asked him.

"I don't know. When I woke up he was gone."

"Gone where?" Sergeant Davidson asked.

"I don't know—just gone."

"He was lying over there last night," pointed Dr. Hanrahan.

"Yeah, and he was complaining about his stomach," added Dr. Stolte.

"Tank, you and Dickerson do a quick search of the immediate area," Sergeant Davidson ordered. "He probably went off to use the bathroom."

From the confrontation the night before, he knew the scientist probably did go into the forest alone. Moreover, his men would probably find him in pieces.

"Don't you think we'd have a better chance of finding him if all of us join the search?" asked Professor Rosenbaum.

"It's too dangerous. The area might contain unexploded ordnances and booby traps, Doc," replied the sergeant.

It was an honest answer. However, because of its likely condition, he didn't want the civilians in the forest when Tanakas' body was found—if it was found.

"Got something over here, Sergeant," Tank yelled through the thick brush. "And it ain't pretty," he whispered to himself.

The scientist approach Tank cautiously, fearful of what he had discovered. Professor Rosenbaum didn't need to see Professor Tanakas' remains. He liked to roll the dice and she knew eventually the odds would catch up to him.

Having met him at Tokyo University while studying ancient architecture, she had known Harry Tanaka for almost ten years. She lived another life when she was with him. They had been on expeditions together in Thailand, Indonesia and in the Amazon. She admired him. He was also spontaneous, courageous, independent and exciting. All the things she wasn't. Professor Rosenbaum sat down and wept.

What was left of the scientist was scattered around a fern tree. There wasn't much. Dr.Stolte noticed an eyeball partially attached to an optic nerve and slightly covered by a gnawed orbital bone. He covered his mouth with both hands, stumbled backwards and vomited on Danny Boy's boots.

"Geez Doc, get a grip on yourself," he scolded.

He tried to clean his footwear with a leaf. TJ stood over a blood-covered patch of soil with remnants of Tanaka's intestines and laughed at his fellow soldier.

"Damn it. These are my best pair of boots."

Lieutenant-Commander Tarkenston picked up a stick and lifted a long tendon partially attached to a fibula.

"What kind of animal did this?" he asked Geri.

"A pack of reptiles probably. My guess is he came out here and was attacked by meat-eating theropods."

"The explosions must have muffled the assault," Lieutenant-Commander Tarkenston added.

"We can't take the time to bury what's left of him. Other carnivores probably have detected the scent by now and who knows what's going to show up next."

Visibly shaken, the scientists and the Special Ops Team members moved on.

Nearing the bellowing sounds of a large group of Placerias resonating from a large plain, the team trudged through thick underbrush. They stood in the safety of the trees as the mammal-like reptiles browsed on tough seed plants growing from the ground. Two huge males tussled, fighting a battle of attrition. Each took turns ramming the other with sharp tusks and each shed blood from injuries inflicted by its rival. Several other skirmishes broke out among the ranks.

"What's going on?" Tank asked. "Are they fighting?"

"I think it's mating behavior," said Geri.

"Just like prairie chickens. Males gather on a mating ground and defend a small courting area. What we're hearing is mostly mating calls," said Dr. Stolte. "The behavior is found throughout nature."

"Are they dangerous?" Lieutenant-Commander Tarkenston asked.

"Animals in larger groups are herbivores while the ones in smaller groups or packs are carnivores. You can also tell by the clawless feet and teeth that these are plant eaters," said TJ.

Amazed, everyone turned and stared at him.

"What? Hey, just a little something I picked up from the Discovery Channel. I love The Dirtiest Jobs and Myth Busters. Anybody else ever watch those shows? They blow up stuff and . . ."

"Dude, why don't you just shut up? You're embarrassing me," said Danny Boy.

"Keep it down, boys," said Sergeant Davidson. "Geri, we'd better keep moving. If it gets as hot as it was yesterday, we had better find water soon."

The temperature did get much hotter as the day wore on. The scientists rested beneath a primitive conifer surrounded by large ferns as Sergeant Davidson's men set up a defensive perimeter. A cool wind suddenly blew through its branches, bathing the team in welcoming relief.

"Feels like rain," said the sergeant.

He removed his binoculars and looked eastward toward a chain of mountains.

"Looks like a storm may be moving in from the east. We'd better get to higher ground."

Dr. Hanrahan and Dr. Stolte sat next to a primitive plant, examing it.

"Can you believe it—Dicrodium. You ever heard of the butterfly effect, Mendel?"

Dr. Hanrahan scratched his stubbly beard.

"Yes and I don't buy it. The idea that a butterfly's wings might create tiny changes in the atmosphere that ultimately causes a tornado to appear is fantasy for science fiction writers, not serious scientists," he replied.

"That's because your example is described in its extreme. Let's try something closer to home. You wake up in the middle of the night to use the bathroom. It's dark and unbeknownst to you, a chair is in your path. You break your toe on the chair, then drive to the emergency room. When you return home, you find your apartment building burnt to the ground and there are fatalities. Years in the future, a time traveler decides to visit your apartment and moves the chair while you slept. The next morning, because you never went to the hospital, you're one of the casualties."

"It's hard for me to believe the universe could be so random, John," said Doctor Hanrahan. "It goes against the laws of physics."

"So you think every action and reaction is part of a universal uniformity."

"Yeah. We're here because we were meant to be here."

"Then I guess the real issue is how will our presence here affect the future," said Dr. Stolte.

"Ladies and gentlemen, time to move," said Sergeant Davidson.

Drenched by a Triassic torrential rainstorm, the team moved on until they reached a huge rocky outcrop alongside the valley floor. A large slab of granite pertruded outward, concealing a small cavity that went a few yards into the interior. Dickerson removed his flashlight and pointed it inside as the team stood around the entrance. Startled by the bright light, a Galechirus, along with its young, scurried out into the rain to the nearest vegetation.

Professor Rosenbaum moved behind Tank for protection.

"I hope nothing else is inside there," she said.

"Are you sure there's enough room for everyone?" Dr. Stolte asked.

He wiped the raindrops away from his glasses.

"Dickerson, go in and take a look," said the sergeant.

"Yes sir."

He handed Harris his weapon, removed his flashlight and held up his knife.

"Just in case he had a friend," said Dickerson, smiling.

After a few minutes, he returned outside.

"All clear, sir. It won't be very comfortable, but at least we'll be dry."

"Great, everybody inside—Tank, you and Harris stay near the entrance."

One by one, the team crawled through the aperture into the evicted reptile's den.

It rained heavily well into the next day. Danny Boy placed canteens outside to collect fresh drinking water while the team finished off the rest of the military rations. The MRE's, a self-contained, flexibly packaged meal, were eagerly consumed.

"We'll have to eat the local plant and wildlife once we're out of these," said Sergeant Davidson.

He tossed another one to Dr. Stolte.

"I'll have a raptor burger and a large dragonfly," said TJ.

Initially met with laughter, his comment brought home a stark reality. The lair quieted as everyone began to realize the seriousness of the situation. No one wanted to say it, but there was very little chance anyone would ever leave the Triassic.

The rain finally stopped. The team set off in search of more comfortable and safer accommodations. They neared a huge rocky outcrop beside a large semi-shallow lake. Primitive insects fluttered about. The afternoon sun battered the valley and everything in it into submission. It glistened off the lake's surface with gusts of hot wind periodically interrupting its stillness. Flourishing around the water's edge, the wind blew lengthy horsetails, forcing them to sing their prehistoric songs. They swayed back and forth, dancing flirtatiously unrehearsed. Recently hatched from a nearby nursery, small primitive lizards scurried about chasing dragonflies. Overhead, Pterosaurs soared, taking advantage of updrafts created by the rising heat. They squawked noisily, announcing the presence of any unwelcome intruders. Several groups of young Coelophysis gathered at the water's edge to quench their thirst. Some took turns as sentries, while others drank nervously. Voicing their disapproval, they screeched boisterously at Pterosaurs gliding over the lake's surface. The flying reptiles skimmed the water with curved beaks, hoping to capture any unsuspecting fish swimming near the surface. Void of any vegetation, the Coelophysis had chosen the area wisely to spot any ambush predator long before it attacked. However, something was watching Coelophysis—and watching closely.

Previously evicted from his pack, a lone Postosuchus lay hidden amongst the tall horsetails. Thanks to a huge skull armed with powerful biting jaws and three-inch long serrated teeth, it was the top carnivore of the age. Heavy-duty armor consisting of rows of plates covered its long back. It watched several inexperienced Coelophysis as they haphazardly attempted to capture primitive lungfish spawning in a semi-secluded tidal pool. Having hunted this area of the lake successfully many times before, it was familiar with the surroundings and the proven techniques used to catch its prey.

Concealed within a huge wall of water, a crocodilian-like reptile burst forth from just beneath the lake's surface. The Phytosaur grabbed a Coelophysis between its formidable jaws, then greedily tried to snare another. Having used the smaller and quicker reptiles as bait, the massive Postosuchus burst through the horsetails with surprising speed. The Phytosaur was unaware of the charging Postosuchus until its powerful jaws had collapsed around its neck. It struggled briefly, releasing the Coelophysis from its mouth. With immense claws pressing down on the ancient crocodilian, the Postosuchus quickly repositioned its bite. The Phytosaur lay on the water's edge, its skull crushed.

"As everyone can see, water attracts predators. We probably shouldn't remain here long," said Professor Rosenbaum.

They spotted a small group of herbivores with long massive bodies, legs, and long necks nearby. Several animals browsed, while others cooled themselves in the shallows.

TJ gripped his weapon tightly.

"Are those dangerous," he asked, nervously.

"I believe those are Plateosaurus. They're plant eaters. I had my doubts at first, but I believe we are indeed in the Triassic period," Professor Rosenbaum replied.

The military men filled their canteens and the group moved on. They followed a stream that fed the lake to the face of an enormous sandstone precipice. Partially concealed by the local plant life, and carved out by a nearly emaciated waterfall, they discovered a cave. Sergeant Davidson removed his binoculars from a pouch and scanned the area.

"This is a good location. We'll set up base camp here. Harris, you, Tank and Dickerson go in and secure the area," he ordered. "Boys, take up defensive positions on that ridge."

Chapter Thirteen
The Atlantis Ring

After entering building LL7 through unimpressive doors, David approached a gate and entered his security code. An elevator carried him to the main security level. With his heart pounding loudly in his chest, he took a deep breath and walked toward the counter. His demons reared their ugly heads.

"What the hell have I gotten myself into this time?" he mumbled to himself.

Images of a chase and death raced through his mind. His legs buckled. David paused for a moment, trying to regain his composure. His jaw tightened as security men at the counter suddenly focused on him. Fighting off the pessimistic forces, he continued toward the security station as the men watched him closely. After exiting a metal detector, he placed his hand on an optical finger scanner. His dossier and security clearance appeared on a monitor in front of one of the officers.

"Good morning Dr. Woodall," one of the security guards greeted.

"Extend your left arm please, and place it there."

He pointed at a black screen embedded in the counter's surface.

David unbuttoned his sleeve, exposing his wrist. The guard retrieved a metallic gun-like, device then wiped Doctor Woodall's skin with an alkaline-based amino pad. The gadget applied a three-inch metallic strip that read and matched David's genetic code. A miniature green light on the strip lit up. He picked up his briefcase, took a few steps forward and placed his security patch under another scanner. His itinerary, security and project clearances downloaded into a Personal Digital Assistant. He looked at the PDA and placed it in his jacket. The Uruguayan artifact wasn't listed.

David proceeded down the hall to another set of elevators and pressed the security patch against a panel causing the door to open. He stepped in, removed the PDA from his pocket and entered the artifact's docket number.

"Information unavailable," displayed on the screen.

Assigned to the Atlantis Ring project, the elevator carried David to level thirty-three.

Made of clay, the ring was a band engraved with a series of geometrical shapes. The shapes consisted of two small triangles and six rectangles of which several had a semi-cylindrical form. At the extremities of the triangles, the ring was perforated and a groove on the inside linked two small holes.

It was discovered in the Valley of the Kings by the Marquis d' Agrain in 1860. Later entrusted to a man named Howard Carter, the several thousand years old archeological find remained in his proprietorship until his death in 1939. However, it was in 1922 that the ring's real mysteriousness emerged. On November 25th of that year, Howard Carter and Lord Carnarvon faced a sealed tomb with the following inscription:

"The wings of death will touch whoever violates the pharaoh's eternal resting place."

They ignored this warning and the two men entered the chamber of Tut Ankh Amon's tomb, son of the sun god and lord of both worlds.

Soon after, Lord Carnarvon began to hallucinate. His condition worsened rapidly and he eventually died, screaming Tut-Ankh Amon's name. His nurse passed away a short time after. Carter's secretary, present at the opening of the sarcophagus, followed. White Evelyne, one of the first to enter the tomb, hung himself. Immediately after seeing the mummy, Aubey Hebert died. Arthur Mace, who first drilled the wall; Lafleur, one of Carter's friends; and Otto Neubert, who investigated eight deaths—all died. Several people died after having lent out for exposition purposes or used objects from the Tut Ankn Amon collection.

The sole survivor of the curse was Howard Carter. He had led the digs from start to finish, made a complete inventory, moved the treasure, and was the first to enter the tomb. When asked how he alone had escaped the curse, he replied, *"I have a talisman that protects me,"* but he would say no more about his good luck charm. It wasn't until after his death, while examining his personal documents, that a mention of a talisman was noted—it was the Atlantis Ring.

#

Technicians were conducting several tests when Dr. Woodall entered the laboratory. A Frenchman shut down an experimental anti-magnetic generator, removed his safety goggles, and walked over to shake David's hand.

"Dr. Woodall, me laisser le dire est un grand honneur."

"Sorry, but I don't speak French," David replied.

He placed his briefcase on a desk.

"It is . . . how you say . . . honorable to be with you here, right now," the student repeated in broken English. "I am big fan."

David became suspicious. His tumultuous childhood manifested itself by way of a subconscious inferiority that provided an ideal breeding ground for accumulating anxiety, self-rejection, and mistrust of others. Over the years, he'd fought to escape those shackles that imprisoned him and in the process, he'd developed a six sense when it came to the unscrupulous and nefarious types.

His father never spoke much, except out of anger. The only way to tell what he was feeling or thinking was by his body movements or facial expressions. Consequently, David read body language very, very well.

"Thank you. I'm sorry, what's your name again?"

David scanned the student's lab coat, searching for a nametag.

"Franco . . . my name is Franco Didier. But everyone calls me Didier."

His English had inexplicably improved.

"I read your paper on dimensions and found it utterly fascinating. Your theory on matter at the subatomic level and how it manifests itself... the relationships between Tran-dimensional particles... groundbreaking."

He had obviously done his homework well; too well for David. He became uneasy.

"I'm glad you enjoyed it, Mr. Didier. Tell me... what school are you attending?"

The Frenchman cleared his throat.

"The Institute Laue-Langevin Grenoble," he answered. "And please, call me Didier. Everyone at the complex calls me Didier."

He removed a pen from his pocket and rubbed it between his fingers. His nervousness didn't go unnoticed. As David glanced at Didier's hand, he quickly returned the pen to his pocket. David recognized this behavior instantly. Suspicious indeed, there was something definitely not right about the Frenchman.

David looked deeply into Didier's brown eyes.

"He's watching you," something whispered in his ear. Getting access to the artifact had become much more difficult.

Didier changed the subject.

"I've run multiple tests on the ring and found several unusual energy readings."

He handed a folder to Doctor Woodall. It contained a history of the artifact, including location found, age, and known or probable extraordinary properties.

"The ring seems to collect and store energy," he continued. He walked over to a machine that fired photons into an ion-filled glass tube surrounding a glass hoop.

David followed behind him, his thoughts clearly elsewhere.

Faced with overwhelmingly psychological discomfort, the human mind tries to protect itself. Sometimes it creates another reality. David's subconscious created a castle to escape the horrific things he saw and the pain he'd felt as a child.

Surrounded by high walls without an entrance, it provided solitude and safety. The middle of the castle contained a tower with a window where he observed the world far away from its brutality. Geri encouraged him to stand and to be fearless in the face of uncertainty. However, woven together with David's qualities like fine tapestry, his dad's destructive idiosyncrasies were still prevalent.

"What? I sorry, what did you say?"

"There were some unusual energy readings from previous tests?"

"No after that."

"The ring collects and stores energy? You okay, Dr. Woodall?"

"Yeah, I'm fine. I have a friend that I'm really concerned about. What kind of energy—kinetic or potential?" David asked, testing him again.

The question was one any college freshman who took a physics course could answer. Didier suddenly recognized David's uneasiness.

"So far it's absorbed about three joules," Didier replied, ignoring the question. "The readings are similar to those taken from the Chalice."

"Good work. Get me your data on the EO spectrograph."

The Holy Chalice was the vessel that Jesus used at the last supper to serve the wine. In 1st Cor. 11:23-25:

"He took the cup when he had supped, saying, 'This cup is the new covenant in my blood.'" Later, Saint Peter, who used it to say mass and eventually took it to Rome, safeguarded it. After Peter's death, he passed the cup on to his successor popes, until Pope Sixtus II in 258. During that time, the Romans persecuted the Christians and demanded that they turned the relics over to the government. Sixtus gave the cup to his deacon, Saint Lawrence, who passed it to a Spanish soldier, Proselius, with instructions to take it to safety in Lawrence's home country of Spain. Unbeknownst to everyone but a few, the Spanish soldier carried a replica. The Chalice sat in a secret vestibule amongst the catacombs,

below the grounds of the Holy See for centuries . . . until The Commission decided to re-invest in it.

David unplugged the vacuum chamber, opened the glass case, and removed the ring. A brilliant multicolored aura engulfed him, blanketing David with an overwhelming sense of euphoria. This went unnoticed by Didier, who sat at a computer station running simulations and analyzing an electro optical spectrograph report. He entered a few hypothetical comments and then downloaded it to his PDA.

"Dr. Woodall, take a look at this," he said as he approached David's workstation.

Startled, David quickly removed the ring from view, resting his hand on his leg beneath his workspace.

"What is it?" he asked.

"Take a look at these readings from the micro spectroscopic analysis I just received from the B lab."

He handed David his PDA, slightly touching his index finger. David noticed a glow at first. He quickly glanced up at Didier, who seemed oblivious to the phenomenon. Expressionless, he watched the aura migrate up Didier's arm and then envelop his body.

Chapter Fourteen
Triassic

The entrance to Pterosaurs Cave, as the team would later label it, was on the nondescript side of a mountain, very unremarkable. As Harris, Tank and Dickerson descended into the cavern, the humidity gave way to a temperate dryness that sucked away the warmth. A natural collapse just inside the entrance blocked the passageway temporarily. With a little ingenuity and a small explosive charge, Harris was able to loosen the stubborn obstruction. After removing the debris, the men continue deeper into the cavern. Several yards later, they came upon a large chamber filled with calcite mounds deposited from dripping water. Some stalagmites were massive and took on a variety of forms from tall, spindly broomsticks to ornate, multi-tiered towers. Each layer, made up of tiny, elongate calcite crystals, oriented roughly perpendicular to the growing surface.

Tank sized up the situation.

"This looks like a good place to set up. There's plenty of obstructions so if something did get in, it wouldn't have a clear run at anyone."

"From the looks of it, this cave goes on for hundreds of meters . . . probably thousands," Dickerson added, shining his flashlight down an extensive meandering tunnel.

After surveying the chamber further, Tank sent Harris to gather the rest of the team.

Outside the cavern, Pterosaurs, which nested on the cliffs high above, soared noisily on the warm updrafts. Danny Boy, TJ and Lieutenant-Commander Tarkenston looked on as the civilian team escorted by Sergeant Davidson examined the plants and rocks nearby. Doctor Stolte picked up a stone and examined it carefully. It was a deep red color with mottling of yellowy brown patches with red colors of iron oxide, mixed with a small amount of clay.

"What ya got there, Doc and where's the sergeant?" Harris asked.

"This? My friend, this is a two-hundred- twenty-million-year-old rock—or at least it will be. Kinda boggles the mind, doesn't it. Sergeant Davidson is down by the large rocks near the patches of ferns," he answered without looking up.

While Dr. Hanrahan and Professor Rosenbaum sat on a limestone platform debating the geographic history of the area, standing on a large boulder, Geri used the opportunity to scan the area with Sergeant Davidson's binoculars.

"I think you're right, Sergeant. This location is close to water and offers adequate protection from predators. We can co-ordinate the search for foreign structures or technology from here. Now the only problem is finding food."

She focused the binoculars skyward at a primitive avian.

"How does roasted Pterodactyl sound?" she jokingly asked.

"In my business, I've eaten just about everything imaginable, Doc. But I don't think I've had the pleasure of dinosaur before."

Harris approached them.

"The cave is secure, sir. We had a little trouble gaining entry, but we've staked out a chamber about seventeen meters inside the entrance."

"Did you encounter any hostiles?"

"No sir. We didn't observe anything in the interior. The place is huge and most of the tunnels are inaccessible because of cave-ins."

They walked back to the cavern's entrance.

"Let's get everybody inside. We'll need wood for a fire and Harris, take the boys and see if you can't round up something for the civilians to eat."

TJ and Danny Boy looked at each other perplexed.

"Like what?" Danny Boy asked.

"Something from the local McDonald's . . . what do you think?" Harris replied sarcastically.

"Screw you, Harris," TJ answered.

"Yeah, screw you . . . Buford!" Danny Boy repeated, mocking his southern accent.

The soldier became agitated. He and TJ tussled briefly.

Realizing the seriousness of the situation, Sergeant Davidson intervened.

Briefed at Langley Air Force Base before the rendezvous with the Argo, his people had seen action all over the world—but nothing could have prepared them for this. The stress was starting to take a toll on them and the sergeant knew it. He took control.

"Break it up. Remain professional, gentlemen," he barked, startling the scientists. "That's an order! Boys, get something for dinner."

"Harris, you're with me . . . firewood duty. Doctor Geraldo, get your people inside."

TJ and Danny Boy headed toward the edge of the primal forest. Tank, dispatched to assist the boys, hurried to catch up with them. They decided not to hunt near the stream because of the possibility of ambushes. TJ and Danny Boy checked their XM8 compact carbine assault rifles. Tank, expecting close quarters combat, removed the Oracle from a leg holster, verified the ammo, and then released the safety on his M249 light machine gun. He had modified it with a grenade launcher, making him a formidable adversary against anyone or anything.

Each man wore experimental tactical camouflage clothing. Sensors located on the garb scanned the surrounding landscape and adjusted the color of the material accordingly. Exceptionally skilled in concealment, TJ recited verses of the TC commandments while applying face paint. Danny Boy joined in.

"Thou shalt blend in with thy surroundings. Thou shalt cover thy face and hands."

"Alright boys, let's go see what's on tonight's menu."

Tank's words caused the boys' adrenaline to surge, heightening their senses. They performed a backhand slapping, forearm hitting, fist punching, hitting their weapons together routine. Tank shook his head.

Special Forces operated in the most difficult conditions and it didn't get any more difficult than this. As they moved deeper into the undergrowth, their training came to bear—search and destroy.

During the Triassic, the first dinosaurs evolved. They were bipedal carnivores or omnivores, small and lightly built, mostly about 10-15 feet long. Some were also very agile and fast . . . some very fast.

Tank, the more experienced of the three, took point as the soldiers stalked their prey. In stealth mode and with senses heightened, they slowly crept through the heavy underbrush, carefully avoiding anything that would give off their position. The prehistoric forest was awash in unnatural noises. To anyone else it would have been extremely unnerving. However, for these very well trained soldiers, it was like hunting a sniper—a sniper with sharp teeth, but still a sniper.

Several meters into the wooded area, Tank suddenly held high a close fist. He turned his head slightly right, trying to isolate the sound of an animal grazing. Danny Boy pointed two fingers at his eyes, held up all five, and then knelt down to examine a large footprint. He then stood up, pointed two fingers at each man and gave a throat-slashing signal. The animal was undoubtedly too large to take down without jeopardizing the men's safety. Whatever was up ahead, ten meters away, received a reprieve. Careful to remain downwind, Tank, TJ and Danny Boy moved on.

Too small for a decent meal, adolescent Coelophysis scurried back and forth through the underbrush. They chased dragonflies and anything else their blade-like serrated teeth could grasp. Preoccupied while chasing a lizard, several ran between Tanks legs, unaware he stood towering above them. Tank being Tank, never flinched.

The men moved several meters east attempting to outflank several other animals in a small clearing. It was risky, but it would be dark soon and extremely dangerous for them to be out in the open. As they methodically advanced toward the targets, Danny Boy heard what sounded like the cry of a child. He carefully pulled back a broad leaf that hid a baby Plateosaurus. The mother, feeding on tender leaves, lowered her huge elongated neck and met him eye to eye. She snorted and then began to sniff him, unable to identify the strange two-legged plant. TJ and Tank, suddenly aware of the situation, froze. The mother inadvertently stepped on the newborn, which let out a cry, causing her to charge. Danny Boy was knocked to the ground, losing his sidearm. A group of Mussaurus hiding together for safety, immersed from the base of the plant in a panic and set in motion a miniature stampede. TJ got off the first shot. Struck by several rounds, the mother bellowed loudly. Other members of her small herd came running to her defense. Danny Boy stabbed and slashed with his combat knife as the Plateosaurus attempted to crush him beneath its feet. Tank joined the fray. Close quarters required him to consult the Oracle. One well-placed hand grenade was enough to disperse the crowd and the Oracle ended the commotion.

The mother Plateosaurus lay dead. Trampled during the upheaval, the baby had also expired. Despite a number of bumps and bruises, Danny Boy pulled through the melee without any serious injuries. TJ and Danny Boy gathered the carcass and carried it back to camp on the firmest branch they could find. Carrying the Oracle in one hand and his M249 in the other, Tank led the way. They headed back to Pterosaur Cave just as the sun began to set.

Chapter Fifteen
USS Argo

Piloting the mildly crippled Cerberus, Lieutenant Mitchell returned to the Argo while Comtac was experiencing difficulties communicating with the team.

"Foxhole to black jackal, Foxhole to black jackal, do you read . . . over? Foxhole to black jackal, Foxhole to black jackal do you read . . . over? Still no response, sir."

"Got anything on remote tracking, Kirk?"

"No sir. One minute everyone was there and the next they're all gone."

"STANCE, run full diagnostic, communications and video array," said Dr. Nashikato.

"Keep trying, Kirk. Bradley, after Lieutenant Mitchell's debriefing, I want the backup security team assembled and ready to deploy," ordered the captain.

"Yes sir. Cerberus secured, sir."

Questioned in Comtac by a DOD official, Lieutenant Mitchell was at a loss to the whereabouts of the team. Dr. Nashikato attended the debriefing and supplied technical support.

He was the real brainchild behind the Argo and her submersibles. He had overseen the construction and implementations of her highly-classified systems, including STANCE the AI. Due to national security, many of Doctor Nashikato disciplines were considered classified. At first glance, one would never know he had an extraordinary analytical mind. Not your typical techno geek, he made whomever he met feel comfortable in his presence. He had an insatiable appetite for knowledge. From the mating habits of the Atlantic Puffin to quasars, pulsars and cosmic strings, Dr. Nashikato wanted to explore it all.

"STANCE, load files EBS 0 dash 9 to 1 dash 3 hundred and access."

Images from the Cerberus downloaded. "READY" flashed on a large video display embedded in the wall.

"File downloads complete, no abnormalities . . . video playback initialized," STANCE announced.

"STANCE, play files external and internal cameras."

Lieutenant Mitchell and the DOD official watched images from the Cerberus displayed on the large screen as Captain Bonar entered the room.

"Did you find anything yet?" he asked the scientist.

"We're going over the video now. So far, AI has found nothing out of the ordinary. Excuse me, Captain . . . STANCE, switch to P in P, 2 cells and scan for any electromagnetic radiation . . . as I was saying, nothing yet. Lieutenant Mitchell left the structure right after she deployed the team. Maybe something relating to their disappearance will show up on the cameras."

"How can people we were monitoring just disappear into thin air?"

"I can say without a doubt that the team is no longer down there. AI can't locate them, but it's reacquired the signal from the unidentified source. Therefore, it rules out some sort of interference. I have several theories, but they're just that right now—theories," replied Dr. Nashikato.

He returned his attention to the images showing on the large monitor.

"I'll be sending the Cerberus back down once I get the authorization. Dr. Nashikato, I'd like you to accompany my security team."

"Captain to the bridge," a voice boomed through an intercom panel located near the door.

Captain Bonar walked over toward the door and pressed a button on the intercom.

"What is it, Riley?" the captain replied.

"Sir, radar reports three bogeys approaching off the starboard bow."

"Go to DSM, Lieutenant . . . condition orange."

The artificial intelligence software, took control of most multi-function consoles relating to command control, communications and combat management systems. Lieutenant Mitchell, the DOD official, Dr. Nashikato and Captain Bonar headed toward the bridge.

"I doubt DarkStar mode will make a difference to the alien's technology," said Dr. Nashikato.

"It's not for the bogeys, Doctor. It's the ships or aircraft that maybe chasing the bogeys that I'm worried about."

Having reached the bridge, Captain Bonar retrieved his binoculars and scanned the horizon. Unable to locate any craft, he contacted Comtac.

"Riley, give me a feed to probe video . . . bridge stations 2B1 and 2C2. STANCE, launch OT probes delta 1 delta 2 DarkStar mode."

Five three-foot tubes rose from a platform on the Argo's aft deck. Aided by the ship's short pulse launch system and with unexpected ease, two missiles from the tubes took flight. The Orion Tomahawks cameras went operational instantly. In receipt of the Argo's active radar, the probes emitted low intensity narrow band lasers to the targets.

"Birds are in the air and on course, sir," acknowledged Riley. "All systems are fully operational."

Despite traveling at high velocity, the images from the Orion probes were exceptional. Dr. Nashikato and the DOD official stood in front of the video displays watching them closely as Captain Bonar continued to scan the skies.

"STANCE, activate delta 2 and 3 gravitational sensors and extrapolate abnormalities. Overlay on screen at maximum resolution," said Dr. Nashikato.

"What are you looking for?" asked the DOD official.

"Comtac radar systems can see the objects because of the Doppler Effect. The Orion prototypes don't have that function yet, so we have to go with the next best thing. The gravitational sensors on the missiles measure the acceleration of light and the reflection time. It then takes that information and formulates an image. See?" said Dr. Nashikato, pointing at a monitor.

The objects briefly appeared on the monitor and without warning, they were upon them.

Circling the ship and constantly shifting positions, they grew brighter then dimmer, then brighter again. As the crew looked on with fascination, the objects changed to a uniformed shape and hue. They came together with a burst of energy that illuminated and slightly rocked the Argo.

Captain Bonar radioed Comtac.

"Initiate maximum stabilizers."

"Maximum stabilizers active," STANCE replied.

Now a perfect square of reflective chrome-colored metal, the object began to spin wildly and then unfold into a connected geometrical Polyhedron—eight then four then one, then one then four then eight. It moved around the Argo slowly, repeating itself as it went. The crew followed it around the deck.

"I think it's trying to communicate," said Dr. Nashikato.

"What makes you say that?" asked the DOD official without moving his eyes from the phenomenon.

"Mathematics . . . it's the universal language. It keeps repeating eight six one and folding back on itself after each forth repetition. It's probably either a dimensional probe or a postcard. Notice the shapes. They're patterns you find in nature. Although they never used any uniform mathematical equations, the Mayans built cities with the same techniques."

The object folded into itself one last time. An intense brightness enveloped the ship, forcing the crew to shield their eyes. With a burst of energy far greater than the first, the Argo rocked severely.

"All stations, condition red!" the captain shouted.

As the crew took their positions, STANCE brought the Argo's starboard arms to bear on the intensifying ball of light. Silently, it collapsed unto itself and disappeared.

"Sir, Comtac is reporting another large bogey two hundred five miles off the port bow and closing—AI locked and tracking."

In the high-tech radar room of the Argo, STANCE activated a red warning light. The AI then accessed real-time satellite imagery within three hundred miles of the ship. It switched from infrared to electromagnetic, then Doppler mode, enhancing the images as it went. STANCE transferred the information to a Comtac station and the ship's bridge.

"Sound battle mode, Lieutenant Mitchell," ordered Captain Bonar. "We won't be caught with our pants down this time."

A brief warning horn sounded; the Argo displayed its splendor. The heliport's aft and forward slowly dropped below deck, replaced by particle cannon platforms. Four conventional missile launchers folded into the Argo, exposing the newly-developed, multiple advanced defense and communication attack targeting systems or MadCats. By sending elementary particles through special fibers in the hull, paint and glass, STANCE activated her new armor. To all conventional means, the Argo was now impregnable.

On the bridge, the captain and his officers peered through binoculars at the approaching craft. As it neared the mighty ship, its massive size became evident. Approximately the mass of three aircraft liners, it silently hovered above the Argo as the AI trained all weapons on it.

"Riley, check the radiation levels," Captain Bonar ordered.

"Particle emissions are normal, Captain."

The alien craft began to glow and move off slowly toward the west, causing the Argo to pitch forty degrees.

"Initializing stabilizers," announced the AI in its remarkable humanoid-like voice.

The large craft then disappeared under the sea.

"Keep your eye on it, Bradley," Captain Bonar radioed Comtac. Launch two MadCats, camera mode only, and transfer video feed to monitors A-8 E-2A."

"Probes away and subsurface, sir," Bradley responded.

The officers stood around the monitors watching as the craft approached the structure. It glowed white, then rapidly flickered white and red.

"STANCE, any increase in electromagnetic output from the RUV's?" asked Dr. Nashikato.

"Electromagnetic readings are within normal operating parameters, Dr. Nashikato," the AI replied.

"Keep a close eye on the radiation markers, Mr. Bradley."

The craft brightness increased, covering the structure with an intense white light and affectively rendering the sensors almost useless.

"Malfunction in the RUV's optical relays, sir," Bradley reported.

"I need a visual, sailor. Get those cameras back on line," the captain snapped.

All monitors suddenly displayed snowy static. Seconds later, they went back to normal operating mode with clear images.

"Good job, Bradley," Captain Bonar praised. Where is the craft? The craft is gone. Where is the structure? STANCE, run full optical diagnostic on deployed RUV's."

"Sir, we have seismic activity coming from the seafloor."

"How massive is it, Lieutenant?"

"Part of the sea floor just uplifted about three hundred forty-nine feet causing the wall of the canyon to collapse. It may create tsunamis. Should we call it in?"

"Send it through proper channels, Lieutenant."

"Sir, by the time the information is distributed, it'll be too late if there's tidal waves."

"Just follow orders, Lieutenant Mitchell—proper channels only."

Two hours later, a tsunami struck Sumatra killing hundreds of thousands.

Chapter Sixteen
Portal

After successfully achieving their objective, Tank, Danny Boy and TJ carried a Plateosaurus carcass back toward Pterosaur Cave. A lone Chindesaurus reconnoiter stalked them from a distance. Having heard the commotion earlier, the inquisitive animal had come to investigate. As the men approach the entranced of the cavern, it hid in an isolated group of ferns trees behind a small rocky outcrop. With cold lifeless eyes, it peered through the leaves, watching silently as the soldiers disappeared into the cave's opening. Tank paused for a moment to take one last look around before entering. Small nocturnal mammals scurried about a few feet from him. He watched as Pterosaurs retreated to their nests, where they awaited the morning sunrise.

The rest of the group had a small fire burning when the men arrived. Cut into small pieces and pierced with sticks, the flames slowly roasted the Plateosaurus remains. Each member had staked out a place on the cavern floor to rest. Because of safety concerns, Sergeant Davidson had his men positioned closest to the entrance, ready to cut down any intruder in a hail of hot lead.

Sergeant Davidson ordered a count of the remaining ammunition and other ordnances while they ate.

"Harris, you take the first two-hour watch. What's your count?"

"Sixty rounds, eight claymores and three Lbs. C-4."

The rest of his men gave an inventory also.

"Dickerson, second watch followed by me, Harris, and then Tank."

"I'll take first watch," said Lieutenant-Commander Tarkenston.

He swallowed hard.

"I'll need a weapon and a couple of hand grenades."

Clearly, he was frightened.

Sure, he was no Special Ops soldier, but he'd graduated from the United States Naval Academy nevertheless. After four years at the "Yard", the life and customs of the naval service became secondary. He'd never been in combat, but he thought of himself as a soldier— and a damn good one at that.

"You sure?" asked the sergeant.

The LC nodded, his hands trembling slightly.

"Alright then, take my sidearm. Harris, give him two frags. Dickerson, give me claymores around the entrance perimeter . . . eight and six meters, and give the LC a couple of HGs. Place four small C-4 charges around the opening, just enough to collapse it and not the entire cavern. LC, whatever you do, don't hit a trip wire while you're out there. Okay, let's get to work."

The men left to perform their given tasks.

"Doctor Geraldo, we'll do a reconnaissance of the area tomorrow," said the sergeant.

"I don't think any structure that contains alien technology is going to be found out in the open. It's more likely to be in a cave, protected from the elements and the local wildlife. We'll follow the base of this cliff for as long as possible and see what we find."

"What's the chance of us getting back?"

"Unless we find what we're looking for, we won't be getting back."

"How's your team holding up?"

"They're scientists. Luckily, they've been preoccupied with their surroundings. It's quite a unique opportunity to study plants and animals that lived over two hundred million years ago. I think they'll be fine for now."

"They need to be more careful, Doc. This is a dangerous place. I can't have them wandering off picking up rocks or looking at leaves, putting everyone else in jeopardy."

Geri leaned forward, resting her head in her hands.

"I know, Sergeant. Frankly, I don't see how any of us will get home alive."

"Let me worry about keeping us alive. You focus on getting us home. Let me tell you a story, Doc."

"In the winter of 2005, eight men and I were running a snatch and grab operation in a village outside of Shindand, in the Herat providence of Afghanistan. It was a dangerous mission. All my men knew that, but they had a job to do. Intel had some Taliban supporters in the area, but none hardcore. We stayed outside the village during the day, hoping to use the element of surprise at night. A group of forty to fifty Al-Qaeda entered the village the night before and we never knew it. The firefight that ensued lasted for hours. I mean rocket propelled grenades, mortars, machine gun fire. They threw everything they had at us, the whole nine yards. Holed up with the Taliban spiritual leader in a compound in the center of the city and surrounded, we were in a bad way . . . and I mean a REAL bad way. I knew deep down, that we probably weren't going to get out of that village alive, but I didn't let my men know that. When they looked me in the eyes, I wanted them to see confidence: The confidence that no matter what, we were going home. We were going to finish our mission and we were going home alive. When you want to do something, Doc . . . all you have to do is believe you can do it and trust yourself. If you don't, you panic, make bad decisions, and people die."

"So what happened? Did you complete the mission?"

Sergeant Davidson stood up and adjusted his earpiece.

"I'm here, aren't I?" He smiled. "I'm going to check on the LC and my men. Try to get some sleep. We have a long day ahead of us tomorrow."

Geri removed a small device from her backpack.

"What's that?" Harris asked.

"It's a GPS device."

"Not like any I've ever seen."

He removed a smaller version from his belt and held it up for her to see.

"Besides, I don't think GPS is going to help us in this place without a satellite."

"This device is a multifunctional prototype. Besides having other capabilities, it's a radio spectrometer with photo-sensors."

"That's great, Doc, but what does it do?"

She moved closer so he could observe the device's display.

"This setting allows me to detect any known radiant or electromagnetic energy and this . . . is the Cryogenic detector mode. The sensors absorb a particle or a photon and deliver a signal whose amplitude is proportional to the energy deposited during the absorption process."

"Yeah, but what does it do? How can it help us?" Harris asked bewildered.

"Hopefully, it'll locate any power source within two hundred and eight feet . . . and our way home."

"Good. Cause I think I left the iron on back at the house," said Harris, seriously.

He cleared a dry area of small stones and dirt. With his finger poised on the trigger, he laid down, his weapon resting on his chest. Geri smiled a warm smile. It startled her. Only moments before it had all seemed so hopeless. She knew she had to hold herself together. Not only were her team and the soldiers counting on her, but also their families. The mission was now a matter of survival. Failure was not an option.

Besides a pack of Coelophysis attacking an old sick Mussaurus amongst the cycads trees, unlike the first, the second night in the Triassic was somewhat uneventful.

Although the cavern lacked the amenities of home, it did provide security.

The floor was painfully uncomfortable. Removing a number of small rocks from beneath her, Geri shifted positions several times. Somewhat more relaxed, her thoughts drifted toward David. Surely, he must be worried sick by now. David was like no man she'd ever met. Sure, he had deep issues like everyone else. However unlike most, he recognized it and struggled to overcome them. He was smart, funny, sincere, himself, and willing to let her be herself. Although he didn't believe in reincarnation, he often joked he'd followed

Geri through many lifetimes just to meet her at this moment. David gave her order and peace. He was able to see things in her she never knew existed. His insightfulness, an ability she lacked, put things in their proper perspectives. They were kindred spirits. She was his ship, while he, her anchor.

With David in her thoughts, Geri rested almost peacefully that night. Two hundred thousand millennia between them couldn't prevent him from comforting her.

High above the cave at dawn, young Pterosaurs squawked hungrily. Occasionally testing their primitive wings, the mature flying reptiles waited patiently for signs of early morning updrafts.

Tank watched as two fluttering hatchlings descended silently, bouncing off a large rock. Convulsing from the fatal plummet, one raised a featherless wing made of membranes of skin. A reptile no more that a foot long appeared from a burrow on the backside of a small rocky outcrop. It flicked its long, slender blue tongue from side to side, tasting the stench of death on the helpless victims. More of its kind joined it. They devoured everything but the boney snouts in a matter of minutes.

"This place is brutal," mumbled Tank.

After observering the spectacle for several minutes, he retreated into Pterosaur cave.

Everyone was awake when he reached the inner chamber. Encouraged by Sergeant Davidson, the scientists consumed the remainder of the Plateosaurus to keep up their strength. After a lengthy discussion, a consensus was reached. The team would split into two groups. One would explore along the precipice's base for any sign of a power source, and the other would retrieve water, firewood and food. This group, it was determined, would carry the majority of the firepower, because it was extremely hazardous. It consisted of Tank, Danny Boy, TJ, Dickerson and Lieutenant-Commander Tarkenston providing tactical, and Mendel Hanrahan, and John Stolte as technical support. Sergeant Davidson and Harris would act as security for the other group while Professor

Rosenbaum and Geri searched for a way home. Dickerson collected his fellow soldier's canteens. Everyone headed toward the entrance.

"Keep radio communications to a minimum," the sergeant ordered.

Tank and his team followed the dried creek bed to the lake. The temperature was already above a hundred degrees by mid-morning. The absence of a breeze made the heat even more unbearable. Primitive animals scurried about feeding in an effort to out-race the pennacle of the scorching rays. Pterosaurs fed their young as bipedal lizards chased large winged insects. Lieutenant-Commander Tarkenston noticed something unusual off into the distance.

"Look over there," he pointed. "There's something shining near the top of that hill."

"Maybe it's the thing we're looking for, or at least a clue," said Tank, looking through his binoculars. "Let's go take a look."

With the tempature steadily rising, ascending the steep hillside was difficult. Except for a few palm-like trees with long, woody trunks and primitive conifers, the landscape contained very little vegetation. Large boulders dotted the terrain. When they reached the general area, the source of the reflection was difficult to locate. The team searched, being careful to stay in visual contact.

"Got something over here," Doctor Hanrahan reported.

He kneeled, brushing away dirt from a partially buried object. After a few seconds of excavating, he held a helmet from a medieval suit of armor in his hands.

"What did you find?" asked Dickerson, looking around cautiously.

"Proof that we were not the first ones here."

"Hey, over here . . . I found something."

Dr. Hanrahan and Dickerson headed toward Doctor Stolte's voice. When they arrived, the rest of the team stood around him viewing the skeletal remains of a medieval knight with a sword clutched by his bones. The armor had scratches and teeth marks along the edges. The sword, painted with thick dried blood, suggested a savage confrontation. Several bones were missing from both the lower and upper half of the skeleton.

"Soldier must have put up one hell of a fight," said Danny Boy.

"This is no soldier and I don't think he died in combat," said Dr. Stolte as he examined the remaining tibia. "He may have perished from a lack of water, but not from an attack. There aren't any large teeth marks on the bones."

"How could he die of thirst this close to a water source?" asked Tank.

"The Triassic was one of the hottest and driest periods of earth history. When he got here, the area may have been in the middle of a drought, so the lake was probaly not even here."

Dr. Stolte lifted the breast plate, exposing an embroidered shirt with sleeves torn from the shoulders.

"E.L.P.P. . . . what does that stand for?" the LC asked.

"Don't know."

Noticing a pocket, the scientist reached into it and removed a laminated identification card. A photograph was embedded in it.

"William Jamison 33-4B994-LL7."

He flip the security badge over.

"Property of the European Laboratory for Particle Physics."

"I didn't think this could get any weirder," said TJ.

"If the guy is from the future, how did he get here? And why was he carrying a sword?"

"Well, two possibilities. He got here the same way we did and either came from medival times, which isn't probable, or he found the armor and sword after he arrived and used it for protection, which is more likely."

Tank radioed Sergeant Davidson about the find. The conversation was overheard by Geri. The sergeant removed his headset and handed it to her.

"Was he carrying anything—anything else out of the ordinary?"

"Nothing Doc. Just your typical knight in shining armor stuff. No wait, got something."

Tank noticed a string around the bones of the skeleton's neck. He knelt down and pulled it as his team watched. The ribs lurched slightly. He wrapped the string around his hand and yanked harder. As if awakened from an eternal sleep, the knight sat up, dislodging an arm bone into the air. It struck the LC in the chest, startling him. He stumble backwards, tripping over a primitive evergreen sapling as TJ and Danny Boy laughed. Embarassed, Lieutenant-Commander Tarkenston rose to his feet. One of the grenades given to him earlier, fell to the ground and rolled a few yards away.

"Careful with that, LC," said Dickerson.

Tank radioed Geri.

"The guy was carrying an metallic orb inside a pouch, Doc."

"Bring it with you so I can examine it," replied Geri.

"Roger that. Out."

He placed the sphere inside a pouch on his belt.

Danny Boy handed the sword to Dr. Stolte. Like a Jacobite commander, he wielded it with ease.

"A Brass Hilted Sword. This weapon helped the Scottish overrun the English at the Battle of Falkirk in 1746."

"That's real interesting, Doc, but it's close to noon," said Tank. "We'd better get to the lake for some fresh water. Dickerson, you got point. TJ, you and Danny Boy bring up the rear. Every animal for miles will be heading for water to cool off by now, so stay alert."

The team headed back downhill using a less grueling route. Although the journey was much easier, the temperature had risen cosiderably. By noon the skies were filled with different species of Pterasaurs soaring on unseen currents high above the valley floor. Because of a drought in an adjacent area, most had flown to the valley from a basin on the other side of the volcano in search of food and water.

An hour of navigating through tree ferns brought the team fifty yards from lakeside. They continued single file to the edge of a glade. A small group of twenty-foot long prosauropods grazed lazily on succulent seed ferns and club mosses.

"Sellosaurus. Probably not dangerous unless they're spooked. I say we try to stay out in the open as much as possible to avoid ambush predators," said Dr. Hanrahan.

Danny Boy inserted a full clip into his XM8 assault rifle.

"Sounds like a plan to me, Doc."

The team reached the lake at the most inopportune time of the day. The sun had risen to its highest point, causing the temperature to soar well above one hundred and twenty-five degrees. Tank brought the group to a halt with a closed-fist hand signal. He put his forefinger to his lips, indicating silence. They stood on the far shore, listening and watching.

"It's so hot, I'm tempted to go for a swim," Dr. Stolte whispered.

An eerily quiet filled the air. The absence of sound was noticeable to all but a lone squawking Pterosaur gliding a foot above the water's surface. Reptiles that usually scavenge noisily along the shore watched it in silence as a prehistoric drama began to unfold. The aerial acrobat drew the teams' attention as it soared gracefully. It circled an area near the middle of the lake, zeroing in on a small school of fish feeding on the surface. Its oddly crested snout and toothy jaws were well suited for grasping fish.

As the Pterosaur opened its tiny teeth-filled jaws to feed, a large crocodile-like reptile broke through the surface with tremendous force. Its mouth agape, it snapped once and missed the Pterosaur. Still ascending vertically, it twisted its massive body in mid air, snapping at the primitive avian twice more. The intensity of the attack sent a shower of water over the flyer, stunning it. It struggled to stay aloft. The Protosuchus made a final attempt to secure its elusive meal as it descended. It grabbed the flying reptile in its jaws and disappeared beneath a wall of water. Panic set in on shore.

"I don't think I feel like swimming anymore," said Dr. Stolte with a blank face.

"Dick, give me the canteens and about twenty feet of trip wire. You and I are going fishing. The rest of you go back and wait in the clearing," said Tank.

TJ and Danny Boy escorted the LC, Dr. Hanrahan and Dr. Stolte back to the glade. They stood quietly observing the prosauropods they had seen earlier.

Weapons to the ready, TJ and Danny Boy paced back and forth, their senses on high alert.

"Have you noticed we haven't see any large herds of grazing animals?" Dr. Hanrahan asked.

"Yes. I thought it might be due to the number the biota can support," replied Doctor Stolte. "Why? Do you have another theory?"

"I don't believe herding behavior has evolved in yet. Look there and over there," Doctor Hanrahan pointed.

Several pairs of herbivors grazed nearby.

"See the mothers with their young. Animals evading a predator illustrates the uncoordinated nature of herd behavior. Each individual can minimise the danger to itself by choosing the location and behavior that is as close to the center of the group as possible. Clearly, there's no evidence of that behavior manifesting itself here."

"Yes, I see what you mean," Dr. Stolte agreed. "They should be in a tighter group for protection and the young should have several adults close by."

At the far end of the clearing, something suddenly spooked a mother Sellosaurus and her young. She bellowed loudly as she hurriely led her calf away from an unseen threat. Other animals headed toward them, setting up defensive positions around their young. Lieutenant-Commander Tarkenston, Dr. Stolte, and Dr. Hanrahan watched, anticipating an attack.

"Look's like I was wrong," said Dr. Hanrahan. "Maybe herd behavior is starting to develop as a defense mechanism."

"I agree. From our observations, I'd say herding is used as a defense, but not as a means of safety."

TJ tapped both men on the shoulder.

"Come on, Docs, we have to move. Let's go, LC."

They withdrew to the relative protection of isolated fern trees. With safeties off, TJ and Danny Boy held their weapons in aiming postures.

Lieutenant-Commander Tarkenston removed the P226 semi-automatic handgun from its shoulder holster. Ill at ease, he retreated against a fern tree.

Moments later, three Postosuchus emerged from the underbrush, chasing a juvenile. Two others joined the pursuit from flanking positions. The Chindesaurus reconnoiter who had followed them all morning, witnessed the melee from a concealed location. Sensing an opportunity for an easy meal, it barked a call for reinforcements. Several Saltopus ran from the glade past Tarkenston's feet. He panicked, shooting twice, missing both times. Danny Boy gave him a stern and unsympathetic glance.

"What the hell are you doing? Keep your head, soldier," he snapped.

Another Saltopus darted between them. Overwhelmed by fear, Lieutenant-Commander Tarkenston ran.

"What's he doing? Where is he going?" Dr. Stolte asked.

"I don't know. Let him go. It's too dangerous to follow. We'll have to find him later," replied TJ.

The LC ran wildly through the underbrush, falling several times. As sharp pointed leaves cut at his face and hands, he dropped his weapon. Something chased him—something terrible.

Stumbling then falling over semi-collapsed cycad, the pursuer slammed a powerful foot atop of the LC's leg and then administered a vicious bite as the rest of the pack arrived. The Chindesaurus reconnoiter reapplied its lethal death grip around both legs. Lieutenant-Commander Tarkenston pounded his fist on the animal's snout as it ripped flesh from bone. Time slowed. Remarkable, he felt no pain and made no sound. The other Chindesaurus attacked. The LC removed a hand grenade and pulled the pin, killing himself and the pre-historic beast in a crimson mist of death. Startled and confused by the blast and flying debris, the remaining members of the pack backed off. An unintended victim of the detonation, the alpha Chindesaurus lay hemorrhaging heavily, missing an extremity. Mortally wounded, it lay shrieking. His rival, a younger male, wasted little time recognizing the good fortune unexpectedly thrust upon him. It attacked the leader, piercing its neck with razor-sharp teeth while clawing ferociously with its dagger-like toes. Other Chindesaurus dragged Lieutenant-Commander Tarkenston's remains toward the nearest fern trees, away from other predators that might have heard the commotion or smelled the blood of their prey and fallen comrade.

#

At the lake, Tank tied five topless canteens, along with a stone, to a long trip wire and then tossed them into the water. They sank immediately. He stared at the air bubbles, hoping they wouldn't attract any awanted attention. Multiple explosions of the handgrenades interupted him. Instinctively, the men hit the ground.

"Was that what I think it was?" asked Dickerson, rising to his feet.

"Sounded like a M2 handgrenade to me," replied Tank.

He radioed the boys.

"TJ, Danny Boy, what's your status?"

"The animals on the far end of the clearing were chased by something and it spooked the LC. Right now he's MIA and we're pin down."

"Stay put. We're on our way."

"Roger that."

Dickerson quickly pulled the canteens in and capped them. Tossing them over his shoulder, he and Tank hurried toward the explosion.

The formation of the super continent Pangaea began the break up during the late Triassic causing huge volcanic eruptions and earthquakes.

As Sergeant Davidson and Dickerson ran toward the glade, the ground began to shake violently. The earthquake loosened large boulders along the valley's walls, sending them tumbling toward the basin below.

Dr. Hanrahan and Dr.Stolte huddled together as they watched the Postosuchus chasing the Sellosaurus and its young. A volcano suddenly erupted putting the entire valley in a state of chaos.

A twelve-foot Chindesaurus burst through horsetails from behind, startling them. It stood there, tilting its head left then right. Confused, the animal took several steps backwards, attempting to compensate for the trembling earth. Danny Boy and TJ pivoted quickly, ready to fire. TJ spun back to a forward position while Danny Boy kept his sights on the carnivore. The animal shrieked, exposing it's bluish pointed tongue.

"It's going to attack. I think it's going to attack!" Dr. Stolte shouted.

"Relax Doc, and stay very, very still. Don't move a muscle," said Danny Boy, calmly.

He slowly reached for a concussion grenade. The Chindesaurus abruptly rushed toward him, knocking him and his weapon to the ground. It then turned its attention toward Dr. Hanrahan who had hidden amidst the foliage a few feet away. The animal grabbed his arm between its jaws. Danny Boy recovered his XM8 assault riffle and fired. One round struck the predator as a large boulder crashed through the vegetation hitting them both. Dr. Hanrahan's body lay amidst the horsetails while the reptile was carried off by the massive projectile.

"Oh my God, he's dead, he's dead," said Dr. Stolte.

"We've got major problems here, Tank," TJ radioed.

"We're almost there," he replied while running. "What's your status?"

"One down, one MIA. Hostiles everywhere."

"Keep your head down. ETA two minutes."
"Roger that. Out."
Tank radioed Sergeant Davidson.

#

The sergeant, Harris, Geri and Professor Rosenbaum evaded falling rocks dislodged from the precipice by the earthquake. They found refuge in a shallow alcove inside the cliff and watched as smoke and magma exploded skyward, darkening the horizon. Lightning flashed inside deadly clouds. Overwhelmed by toxic gases, Pterosaurs fell from the sky.

"Let me see your binoculars," Geri asked Sergeant Davidson as Tank's voice came through his earpiece.

"We got casualties, sir," said Tank as he picked up a semi-automatic handgun from the ground. To the left, a boot and partial lower leg lay close by.

"Sergeant, tell your men to get back to the cavern right away," Geri said alarmed.

"Tank, stand by. Why—what's the emergency, Doc?"

"There," she pointed. "If that volcano erupts any further it'll rain hot ash all over the valley floor."

"Tank, get everybody back to the cave ASAP. I'll explain when you get there."

Automatic weapon fire erupted through the sergeant's earpiece.

"Roger that."

After a few moments, the quake subsided. Smaller stones continued to fall from the cliff with less frequency.

Geri, Sergeant Davidson, Harris and Professor Rosenbaum beat a hasty retreat back to Pterosaur Cave.

#

"Where's the Doc?" asked Tank as he and Dickerson knelt beside Danny Boy and TJ.

"He's dead," replied TJ, pointing his XM8 assault rifle at the horsetails. "The LC got spooked and ran off."

"He's dead, too," replied Tank. "We found what's left of him about forty meters back. We've been ordered back to the cave pronto, so here's the plan. Dick, throw a couple of concussion grenades about twenty degrees left and twenty degrees right, twenty meters out. Then concentrate your M4 Carbine at twelve o'clock to open up a clear path. The rest of us will lay down suppressive fire on our flanks and to the rear. That should cause any animals close by to disperse. After I give the signal, I want everybody moving double-time. Danny Boy, you take point."

Tank looked into Dr. Stolte's eyes and placed his hand on his shoulder.

"Doc, you ready?"

"Yes," Dr. Stolte nodded.

"Good. Alright then, let's do this. Okay boys, Dickerson . . . on three. One, two, three!"

Gunfire and explosions reverberated through out the valley. Leaves, dust and smoke filled the air around the men. The ordnances frightened or killed every animal within a thirty-meter radius, creating a safe corridor.

"Cease fire, cease fire. Everybody—go, go, go," barked Tank.

Periodically firing into isolated areas of brush and trees, the group beat a hasty retreat toward Pterasuar Cave. The pack of Chindesaurus followed at a safe distance.

Dr. Stolte stumbled then fell, impaling his thigh on the bone of a large reptilian skeleton.

"Get up," barked Tank.

For the first time, the sound of urgency was in his voice. It made the boys uneasy. Tank looked to his six. Two of the carnivores attemped to outflank them on the left. Four more reptiles were hot on their heals. TJ lifted Dr. Stolte by the arm.

"We got company. Defensive positions," yelled Tank, firing his grenade launcher.

The men formed a protective circle around Dr. Stolte.
Dickerson unloaded a M4 Carbine clip into the brush.
"I'm out."

He removed his sidearm and MPK knife, ready for hand-to-hand combat. The Chindersarus scattered then regrouped. Caustiously, they continued to advance. Danny Boy knelt next to Dr. Stolte.

"This is going to hurt, Doc—probably a lot."

The scientist grimmaced as Danny Boy pulled the bone from his leg. Blood squirted from the wound.

"Looks like it nicked the artery. It's not bleeding too badly though. You'll be alright."

He ripped the sleeve from the scientist's shirt and wrapped it around his thigh.

"Come on, we gotta get going," said Danny Boy, lifting him to his feet.

TJ let loose a barrage of automatic weapons fire from his XM8 assault rifle, wounding one of the reptiles. It shrieked a hellish sound, sending a chill down Dr. Stolte's spine. He covered both ears with his hands.

"I'm out," TJ yelled over the explosions.

He too removed his sidearm.

With Danny Boy assisting the injured Dr. Stolte, the men reached Pterasaurs Cave. The Chindersaurs pursued.

Tank stood by the entrance, firing more grenades.

"Quickly, everyone in," he yelled over the noise from the explosions.

TJ trippped and fell, the top of his nose touching one of the tripwires. He slowly inched backwards, careful not to set off the device.

The Triassic was an unforgiving place. The reptiles were immediately on him. He groaned as serrated teeth clamped down on the hand holding his weapon. The bipedal carnivores dragged him several feet, shaking him like a rag doll. A smaller less experienced predator attempted to bite TJs foot as it swung wildly in the air. Danny Boy handed Dr. Stolte over to Dickerson.

"Get everyone in and get ready to blow the entrance," he yelled.

"You can't go out there," said Tank, grabbing his arm.

"That's my friend; the only real friend I've ever had. Now let go of me."

He took the sword from Dr. Stolte's hand and ran toward TJ.

"Hold on, buddy, I'm comin," he said loudly.

Surpised by the soldier's boldness, the primitive beasts ceased their attack and backed off.

"Haw! Haw!" Danny Boy yelled, confusing them further.

He swung the sword in the air wildly.

Careful not to lose sight of the animals, he reached TJ who had lost several fingers in the struggle, and knelt next to him. Hissing, the ferocious reptiles paced back and forth like caged lions, trying to muster up enough courage for another attack.

"How ya doing, J—can you walk?" Danny Boy asked, looking down at his friend.

A Chindersaurus quickly leapt through the air feet first at Danny Boy, who drove the sword into its abdomen. The others moved closer.

"I'm not going to make it, DB. Here, take these."

TJ removed his dog tags and handed them to Danny Boy.

"You're not done yet, buddy," replied Danny Boy.

Sword in one hand and his MPK knife in the other, he stood up ready to face the inevitable.

As the predators slowly advanced, a burst of automatic weapons fire hit the ground around them. The Chindersaurus once again retreated.

"Hurry up and get him on his feet. That won't hold them off long," said Sergeant Davidson as he approached the boys.

Harris and Dickerson moved between them and the reptiles, firing their weapons.

"Short bursts only. Save as much ammo as possible," said Sergeant Davidson.

He helped TJ to his feet.

"You okay, soldier?"

"I've seen better days," said TJ, grimacing.

"Just imagine the stories you"ll be able to tell your grandchildren, huh?"

The men retreated back to the cavern.

"Tank, you and Dickerson rewire the explosives at the entrance," Sergeant Davidson ordered. "Denonate a smaller charge to partially collaspe the entrance to make it difficult for those things to get in. I want everyone to do a weapon and ammunition check right away. Harris, you have first watch. What's your count?"

"Thirty-eight rounds, three concusion grenades and five claymores, sir."

"Tank."

"Except a couple of rounds for the Oracle, I'm out."

"Dickerson."

"Ten rounds sidearm ammo. Five claymores. A pound of C-4."

"TJ, Danny Boy."

"Out."

"Twenty-two rounds and one greneade, Sergeant."

"Why didn't you fire ealier?"

"Weapon jammed, sir. I'll be sure to report it to the armory commander when we get home."

"Well, that was either one of the bravest things I've ever witnessed or the dumbest. I haven't decided yet," said the sergeant.

"Harris, you and Dickerson gather firewood. Grab what you can close by. Tank, you, me and Danny Boy will reinforce our defenses. We're going to make this place impregnable. Lets go . . . it's going be a long night."

Dr. Stolte rested near the rear of the chamber. He stared at the wall, his eyes and mind millions of years away.

"What about him?" Tank pointed.

"He'll be alright. He's just in shock."

The soldiers headed out of the cavern.

TJ sat on the cavern floor holding his dog tags. He dropped them as Geri tighten the bandages wrapped around his badly mangled foot and hand.

"Easy Doc," he grimaced. "That's my ass-kicking foot."

"You'll be alright, soldier. You'll be on your feet in no time."

The multifunctional device in her backpack began to beep. She walked over and retrieved it.

"What ya got, Doc?"

"Looks like an energy signature," she replied, studying the readings.

She moved the instrument back and forth trying to isolate the source.

"It's coming from back there," she said, pointing toward the back of the chamber.

Geri removed her flashlight from the backpack and turned it on. It penetrated the darkness, illuminating a dark passageway.

"Wow," she whispered to herself. "That wasn't here yesterday."

The corridor's ceiling was partially collasped and in its current condition, almost impassable. Stepping over rubble and sqeeezing through small opennings, Geri slowly continued forward. She reached a chamber somewhat exposed by the earthquake. Dislodged by the strong tremors, a large area of ceiling partially rested on the cavern's floor. Unable to advance any further, she peered in.

Near the middle of the chamber lay a group of stones, eight in the outer circle and four in an inner. In the middle of the four large stones stood a platform with symbols located on the top and sides. The readings from the device were off the chart. She instantly recognized the symmetry of the stones as the same as those found in the underwater structure.

"Bingo."

Unable to move any of the debris, Geri headed back toward the main chamber for help.

#

Outside the cave, the soldiers finished collecting wood and resetting their explosives. A Chindesaurus moved to their flank in the midst of the trees.

"I've got movement thirty-five meters at your one o'clock," said Sergeant Davidson through his headset. "What's your status, Tank?"

"A couple more to go."

"Danny Boy—how are you doing?"

"Almost there, Sergeant," he replied, brushing dirt over a fragmentation grenade.

The sergeant fired a round from his grenade launcher into the trees. He pressed his radio microphone twice, alerting Harris and Dickerson to return from wood gathering duty.

"That's it. Everybody back inside—looks like there's something brewing."

Harris and Dickerson piled the firewood behind a large stalagmite that had fallen over against the wall.

"Dickerson . . . are the charges ready at the door?"

"Yes sir."

"Blow it. Make sure you leave enough room for us to get out, but not enough for anything to get in . . . got it?"

"Yes sir."

"Everybody go to the back of the cavern. Where's Geri?"

"She got a signal and went back there to check it out," replied TJ.

"Okay Doc, you should be fine right where you are," said Sergeant Davidson.

He stared at Dr. Stolte for a moment, waiting for a response.

The scientist sat against the wall, expressionless, staring into dark emptiness.

"Shock," said Tank. "He'll snap out of it sooner or later."

He and Danny Boy helped TJ to his feet and moved him to the farthest wall.

"Ready Sergeant," Dickerson called out.

He withdrew behind a large round stone, unraveling a long wire.

"We're all set back here. Go ahead."

"Okay then, here goes nothin' . . . Fire in the hole!"

The explosion collapsed a large piece of the ceiling and part of the entrance wall. A plume of smoke and fine dust rushed out the cave's opening. Sergeant Davidson went forward to inspect Davidson's handiwork.

"Perfect. That went better than I expected," he said, waving the dust cloud from his face.

The detonation had cut the entrance space to a quarter of its original size.

"At least the bigger ones won't be able to get in."

Geri returned from the long dark corridor.

"What was that? What was that noise?" she asked.

"That was the sound of a good night's sleep, ma'am," replied Dickerson.

"I don't want to get everybody's hopes up, but I think I've found what we were looking for," said Geri.

"You found it? Where?" asked Professor Rosenbaum.

"It's in a chamber several meters down that corridor," she said and pointed with her flashlight. "I couldn't get through because of a partial cave-in."

Explosives began detonating outside the cavern.

"Tank, you and Harris stay up top. Dickerson, Danny Boy, you with me," said Sergeant Davidson. "Let's see if we can move the obstruction so we can get the hell outta here. And Tank—nothing gets in."

The soldiers moved into position as explosions echoed outside. There was barely enough room between the debris for the men to aim and fire their weapons.

"Be careful with your ammo," said Tank. "Try and squeeze off one round at a time. William Prescott at the Battle of

Bunker Hill said, *'Don't fire until you see the whites of their eyes.'* Well, don't fire until you see the blue of their tongues."

Harris chuckled.

"Man, am I glad that meteorite killed all of the dinosaurs."

"That was an asteroid not a meteorite."

"Yeah, whatever—anyways, it's going to be next to impossible to get a good shot from this position. Did you see that? One just ran by. Man, these things are smart—too smart."

He fired off a couple of rounds.

#

Geri, Dickerson, Professor Rosenbaum, Danny Boy and Sergeant Davidson slowly crept back through the dark tunnels and passageways. Columns of stone and large pillars decorated the floor. In a smaller corridor behind fallen debris, a small muddy puddle held stone lily pads that seemed to float on its surface.

"Looks like we have access to water," said Geri. "I must have missed this the first time I came back here."

They continued down another narrow passageway, reaching the chamber Geri had discovered earlier.

Sergeant Davidson removed his weapon and laid it against the wall. He walked back and forth peering at the ceiling.

"We shouldn't have a problem with a cave-in if we move it. You guys take that side and on the count of three, push forward."

Along with silt and dust, the large stone slab fell to the ground and shattered into several smaller pieces.

"That was easy," said Dickerson.

He retrieved his weapon.

Geri stepped into the chamber, taking readings as she went.

"Same energy signature," she exclaimed smiling. "If I can get the technology to work, we may be home soon."

"Yes!" said Danny Boy, pumping his fist excitedly. "We can finally get out of this hell hole."

"Geri, you and Professor Rosenbaum stay here and see if you can get this thing to work. Dick, help her out. DB and I will go back and get the rest of the team," said the sergeant.

#

Back at the entrance, the battle between monsters and man raged on. While some animals inadvertently activated tripwires setting off explosions, others scavenged their carcasses. Finally, the explosions stopped. The scene outside Pterosaurs Cave was a picture of unattached heads, legs and arms of primitive reptiles. However, none belonged to the Chindesaurus. They had started a stampede through the battlefield and had lured larger predators to chase them into the chaos. Now that the danger was over, they were back.

They scurried back and forth in front of the cavern entrance, forcing Harris and Tank to take fleeting shots at them.

"You know, I remember this girl I met on the beach in Cancun about three years ago while on R&R. She was very good looking, but that's not what attracted me to her. She was different, down to earth and confident—the only person that I've ever met that was able to disarm me from the inside. Know what I mean?"

"If she was so great, why didn't you marry her?"

"Because I was afraid."

"You? You're not afraid of nothing," said Harris.

"I wasn't afraid of her. I was afraid to let my guard down—to be vulnerable. You know, Harris, everybody is running from something whether they're willing to admit it or not. When I get back home, I'm through running."

Harris stared at Tank for a moment. They had known each other for years, yet never had Tank spoke of anything so personal. He didn't know how to respond.

"I'm out," he said, removing his MPK knife.

"Yeah, me too," said Tank, pulling the Oracle from its holster.

The lull in weapons fire further emboldened the reptiles. Spearheaded by the dominate Chindesaurus, they rushed the cavern's entrance. The Oracle fired, temporarily dispersing the animals. Tank fired again, grazing the largest of the eight. He placed the weapon back into its holster.

"I'll let her do the dirty work in case they get in," he said to Harris with a wink.

He removed his knife.

Regrouped, the Chindesaurus were back on the doorstep. Shrieking and clawing feverously, they pressed their snouts into any open crevice between the fallen debris. Tank and Harris stabbed at reptilian feet and claws as they penetrated past the fallen rocks.

"If this wasn't so serious," said Harris, lunging and swiping at an evading snout, "it would be funny."

"Yeah, I know what you mean," replied Tank, stabbing a scaly claw.

The animal shrieked, retrieving its arm.

"Kinda reminds me of a game we use to play as kids," he continued, swiping at reptilian flesh. "We'd sit on the porch and shoot at gophers as they poked their heads out of holes. Boy, what I would give for the good old days."

The Chindesaurus inexplicably retreated.

"What happened? They're leaving," said Harris.

"I don't know, but I don't like it. Maybe they've had enough."

He peered through a gap between the fallen debris. Dust fell from the roof of the cavern, striking him on the head. He looked up.

"Cover your head. It's an earthquake!"

The ground shook slowly at first, then violently. A large stalactite fell from the ceiling, striking Harris. The earthquake opened up a larger hole at the entrance and the Chindesaurus quickly took advantage of it. A subordinate was the first to squeeze through the new opening. It stumbled over Harris, falling. The Oracle was ready before the prehistoric beast could recover. Tank fired. At close range, nothing could withstand a round from the weapon. The ancient theropod was no exception. Killed instantly, it fell to the ground without a whimper. The rest of the pack tried squeezing through the opening all at once causing a bottleneck. Lying injured on the cavern floor, Harris stabbed feverishly at the evaders. Blood flowed from a severe gash to his eye. He tried wiping it away with his hand.

"Get everybody outta here," he yelled. "I'll hold them off."

"I'm not leaving you here to die, buddy," said Tank.

The Oracle fired two more volleys, mortally wounding the smallest of the animals. The Chindesaurus retreated.

"You have to get them out, Tank. You can come back for me later."

Tank helped TJ and Dr. Stolte to their feet and followed the passageway taken by Geri and the others.

Chapter Seventeen
The Kronotus Sphere

In the midst of gently rolling hills that surrounded Lake Zurich as well as on the Linth Plateau, the commission had numerous clandestine facilities. Lake Zurich linked the City of Zurich with Rapperswil, the City of Roses. The journey from the city by train or car usually took a good half hour, while the trip by boat was somewhat more leisurely. Security concerns, however, all but negated the second alternative.

After obtaining Didier's access ID card and the location of the Uruguayan artifact, David took the elevator to section 2035B. Because of the quantity and significance of relics sent to the assessment center, a security station guarded against any unwelcome guest or theft. Still wearing the Atlantis Ring he had stolen earlier, David exited the elevator and walked right to the security desk. He swiped his badge through a card reader as a security guard looked on expressionless.

"Dr. Woodall," acknowledged the officer, looking at the monitor then up again. "You don't have clearance to be in this area."

She removed a red cordless phone from a base on top of the desk.

"I'm going to have to call this in."

"Wait a minute," said David, grabbing her wrist."

The mystical effects of the ring immediately overcame her.

"Try this one."

He handed her Didier's access card.

Engulfed by an aura, the security guard ran the card through the scanner.

"Professor Didier, good to see you again," she greeted. "What brings you to our little corner of the universe?"

"I'm looking for an artifact. The one found in Uruguay. I was told it may be in a lab on this floor."

The guard moved to a computer terminal and began to type.

"Do you know the A.L.D. number?" she asked without looking up.

"A.L.D. number?"

"Yeah . . . assigned listed docket number. Come on, Professor, stop pulling my leg," she said, smiling. "You're such a kidder."

"Yeah, that's me, always joking around," said David.

"I do have something from Uruguay scheduled in sky lab. Looks like the Kronotus Sphere. It's there now."

"Good. I think that's what I'm looking for," said David.

He headed down the corridor.

"Excuse me, sir. Excuse me," a security guard yelled, running after him.

David took a deep breath. Surely, he'd been found out. He ignored the man's voice.

"Sir . . . sir," called the officer, coming closer.

Unable to discount him any longer, Dr. Woodall slowly turned around.

"You forgot your ID card Professor Didier."

"Thank you," said David with a sigh of relief.

Since he'd never encountered this guard at the security station, David wondered why the officer had not discovered his deception. He took the ID card and continued down the hallway. Because of unknown effects, he decided not to use the mysterious ring again unless extremely necessary.

After passing several doors, sky lab came into view. He stood at the door, took a deep breath, then swiped the card through the reader. A green light lit on the display, then red, then green again. *"Enter security code"* blinked on and off on the display. He moved closer and pressed 8-1-1-5-5-6-9. The lights flashed a second time, green, then red and red again.

"Oh shit," he mumbled. "Wrong code."

He pressed the keypad again—*eight one one five five six nine*. The red light blinked rapidly. David took a step backwards and put both hands on top of his head. He looked down the corridor and began to pace.

"I can't believe I've forgotten his password," he whispered.

He tapped his forehead, trying to access his memory.

"The alarm will sound if I enter the wrong security code three times. Think, think, think, what is the code—what is the code—8-1-1-5-5-6-9—8-1-1-5-5-9-6, nope, that's not it, 8-1-1-5-6-5-9, no, no, no!"

He paced again.

"Guess I'll have to chance it."

Biting his lower lip, he stepped forward. He swiped the card a third time, then stared at the keypad for a brief moment. David brushed his hand across his chest and then blew on his fingers like a skilled safe cracker. He slowly moved his forefinger toward the keypad. It was a millimeter away when the door suddenly opened. Two Chinese technicians stepped out and headed down the corridor. Relieved, Dr. Woodall went inside.

With multiple sub labs, the sky lab was the biggest and most versatile in the facility. It contained all types of scientific equipment from super compressed particle accelerators to multiphase generators to experimental investigational multimillion-dollar machinery. Through an elaborate use of subterranean shafts, tunnels and advance optics, the commission was able to open up the lab to the outside world. It was a physicist's dream. All relics and artifacts came through sky lab doors for analysis eventually.

David removed his PDA and placed it in a cradle, synchronizing it with the nearest terminal. He typed several keys and then entered information into his device. He watched as images of the artifact, now known as the Kronotus Sphere, downloaded with all current research data. He removed the PDA from the cradle and quickly scrolled through it.

"I was right, it is a time displacement device," he mumbled to himself.

He read on.

After technicians bombarded it with rare particles from high-energy nuclear reactions, the object had changed shape to a sphere. A subsequent analysis revealed an increase in negative energy density and in exotic materials. Dr. Jamison also observed a small distortion of space-time around the artifact as it transformed.

After scanning through the rest of the data, David returned the PDA to his pocket and headed toward the multiphase temporal displacement generator. Previously owned by the Department of Defense and stored at a military base in Nevada at the southern end of a large dry salt flat called Groom Lake or Area Fifty-one, the commission had taken ownership of it in a brazen daytime operation.

In a sub lab, he found a woman conducting tests on the artifact. David gathered himself and approached her.

"Nice day, isn't it," he addressed her, searching for an identification tag.

He extended his ringless hand.

"I'm Dr. David Woodall."

Preoccupied, the woman turned slowly and peered over her wire-framed glasses.

"My name is Doctor Brahms—Dr. Hilda Brahms," she said with a heavy German accent.

"So Dr. Brahms, what are you working on?" David asked.

"The Kronotus Sphere . . . it's a most remarkable piece of technology."

David peered into the holding chamber. The artifact was hardly recognizable since he'd last seen it in its rectangular form. The hieroglyphic symbols and hue had changed completely. In his report to Dr. Jamison, David had theorized that the object was able to manipulate space-time, but of course he had shrugged it off as a delusional fantasy.

"Take a look at the readings from the latest test on the monitor. I've narrow the external forces influencing the object to a few hundred probable particles, some of which our current technology can't identify."

"Is that a fact," replied David. "Where is your current data?"

She handed him a laptop PDA.

"Tachyons," he said softly after reviewing the numbers.

"I'm sorry, what did you say?"

"Nothing—I see you exposed it to cosmic rays."

"Yes, I did—and I achieved some of my better results from the process."

Dr. Jamison entered the lab.

"Woodall, wot 're ya doin' 'ere?"

"We were just discussing the Kronotus Sphere. I had some new ideas I wanted to try, so I came here to see how the investigational process was going."

"Eaven and hell—what ideas?"

"Well, by increasing cosmic ray particles to an energy output level roughly about five hundredth that of the universe, twelve point seven billion years after nucleosynthesis, we should have a better understanding of the artifact's properties."

"You wanna subject the blooming sphere to radiation equal to that of the bleeding Damien Hirst current ban?"

"Yeah—I think that's what I just said."

Dr. Brahms raised her objections.

"Eine minute, warten. Eine Zustimmung ist für Verteilungen solcher großer. Mengen Betriebsmittel auf einem Projekt notwendig."

"What did she say?" David asked Dr. Jamison.

"I said an approval is necessary for allocations of such large amounts of resources on one project."

"Well I say, I'll sign off on it then," Dr. Jamison said, abruptly.

He picked up a telephone and ordered several labs temporarily shut down.

"What-oh Dr. Brahms, mustah on with it."

She opened a draw and removed three pair of dark goggles.

"Here, keep these on until the reading on the monitor reaches zero."

They walked up a short staircase into an observation chamber. Dr. Brahms typed on the keyboard, lowering the containment glass. Multiple tubes slowly descended from the ceiling, encasing the object in a translucent octagonal residence of glass. She pressed more keys, activating the fusion reactors. A soft humming sound reverberated throughout as a brilliant white light suddenly overshadowed everything in and outside of the containment area.

"Well I say, it's dishy, absolutely dishy," said Dr. Jamison.

Staring at the slowly expanding illumination, he opened the door and walked outside the observation chamber. Papers blew about the room.

"Goodness me, it's magnificent!" he yelled over the howling wind.

The brilliance drew him like a moth to a flame.

"What are you doing?" Dr. Woodall shouted.

Mesmerized, the scientist continued forward. Silver sparks flashed as the illumination consumed him.

"Shut it down! Shut it down!" David yelled.

The generator grinded to halt, deactivating the reactors. The brilliance disappeared with a whoosh, taking the renowned scientist with it. Dr. Brahms screamed.

"Where is he? What happen to Dr. Jamison? He's dead, he's dead," cried a horrified Dr. Brahms.

#

The brilliance surrounding Dr. Jamison transformed into total darkness. As it gradually lifted, he attempted to get his bearings. Unfamiliar sounds and the smell of sulfur were his first clues that he was no longer in the lab. When the darkness had finally lifted, he found himself standing amidst a group of horsetail reeds and primitive cycads.

#

Dr. Brahms picked up a phone to notified Dr. Willoughby of the unfortunate circumstance.

"Calm down, Dr. Brahms. Tell me exactly what happened."

"We were trying to recreate conditions before nucleosynthesis by bombarding the artifact with high-intensity cosmic rays. The resulting exotic particles, we believed, would give a more accurate indication of the object's characteristics."

"That would have required my approval for that amount of energy alone. Who gave the okay for it?"

"Dr. Jamison. I heard him make the phone call. It was Dr. Woodall's idea."

"He made no request," said Dr. Willoughby.

He accessed David's dossier on his computer screen.

"Dr. Woodall is not even scheduled for that area."

Dr. Brahms turned to look at David. As their eyes met, he knew instantly something was wrong.

"Listen to me very carefully. Keep Dr. Woodall in the lab. I'm sending a couple of men to pick him up for questioning," said Dr. Willoughby.

David headed toward the door.

"It's too late. He just left," said Dr. Brahms.

Dr. Willoughby reached under his desk and activated a silent alarm, effectively putting LL7 on lockdown.

"Dr. Brahms, I want you to report to the security station near the elevator. They will instruct you on your next course of action."

"Yes sir."

Her hands trembled as she hung up the phone.

David exited the lab and entered the corridor. He was surprisingly calm considering security officers were surely searching for him. He looked left and then right. Approaching footsteps echoed from down the hall. His breathing increased, creating a strange tempo between the pace of his pursuers and the rhythm of his beating heart. David hurried left. Smaller labs, offices and other rooms decorated the corridor, each requiring a security code to access. He quickly tried them all. After several hundred feet, he reached an unlocked door near the end of the corridor. It led down a smaller hallway toward a well-lit stairwell. He peered through a small window on the door as security personnel and two other women took Dr. Brahms away in handcuffs. David headed for the stairs.

#

Inside the building's operations center, security personnel scanned through images supplied by hundreds of close circuit video cameras positioned throughout the facility.

"Colonel, there's been a security breach. Get some of your men to the west side of the building," ordered Dr. Willoughby over a handheld radio. "Dr. David Woodall was spotted near stairwell C. I want you and your men to keep a low profile and escort him to my office. Do not allow him to leave the area. Do I make myself clear?"

Depending on the level of research, the commission sometimes deployed an elite team of commandos on site at specific clandestine facility. Led by a former Ukrainian Air Force officer, Colonel Aleksey Prokopovich and his men guarded against any incursion or infiltration by hostile forces at LL7. A suspicious man who distrusted anything or anyone American, the colonel was a leftover from the heydays of the Cold War. He believed in the heavy-handed approach and practiced it unhesitatingly.

"Crystal sir," responded the colonel.

He radioed his men at the gate.

"Nobody gets in or out without my direct order."

#

In the stairwell, David started his climb to the surface. He had taken a few steps when he turned and headed back downward.

"They'll be expecting that," he said to himself.

Several flights down, he exited. David peered through the small window on the door. Scientists and technicians went about their normal activities unaware of the current calamity. He stepped into the corridor and stared at a video camera mounted on the wall. He turned away quickly, attempting to hide from its cold and penetrating stare.

"I think we got him, sir. A camera on J level section C8 just picked him up near the stairs," one of the security personnel reported.

"Good, contact Colonel Prokopovich and tell him to get some of his men down there right away," said Dr. Willoughby. "And notify the guard station on that floor and tell them to discretely seal off the area."

David hurriedly moved down the corridor toward the elevators. Several voices around the corner and out of view suddenly impeded his path to freedom. Colonel Prokopovich stood before security personnel distributing photographs of David.

"Gentlemen, security has been compromised. The subject, a Dr. David Woodall, is a собака а шпигун and a шпигун . . . a dog, a spy, and a traitor. He is to be taken alive for interrogation. You two take up positions near the elevator. You take the east side and you the south. You, you come with me. We are going to look in every room and laboratory on this level. The rest of you will do the same. Start in the stairwells and do floor by floor searches down five levels to the student dormitories."

David turned and headed back toward the stairs. One of the colonel's men opened the stairwell door, startling David. He ducked inside a nearby door well. The commando walked toward him, periodically tapping his stun stick against the wall. David listened carefully as the sound grew louder. Several desperate scenarios swept through his mind.

At least I'll have the satisfaction of knowing I did something to try and save Geri, he thought to himself.

He searched his pockets, looking for a weapon. Between the rhythmic taps of the stun stick against the wall, he noticed his breathing had become heavier and louder. He held his PDA high in his hand ready to strike, just as the security door suddenly opened behind him. Didier grabbed David by his collar and pulled him inside. He held his index finger to David's lips.

"Keep quiet," he whispered. "Follow me."

They walked to an area in the back of the supply room where Didier had removed an air vent. He handed David a wristband with small electronic chips imbedded throughout it.

"Here, put this on."

"What is it and who are you?"

"Among other things, it's an electronic jamming device. And don't touch me with that ring again."

"What? How did you know about that? Wait, who in the hell are you? And why is it you can speak perfect English now?"

"I thought your job was to answer questions, Dr. Woodall—not ask them," said Didier. "Besides, it's not important who I am. Right now, I just need to get you out of here. When you're out—go directly to the airport. There's a ticket for you in the name of Christopher Kryczek at gate twenty-nine. Whatever you do—don't go to any hotel."

"I'm not going anywhere until I get some answers," said David. "How do I know you're not working for them? You sure seemed to be in the lab."

"Dr. Woodall, if we're caught we're both dead."

David stood his ground.

"Okay David. Dr. David Woodall—born in 1975, Atlanta, Georgia, to Sarah and an uneducated alcoholic father, Thomas Woodall—ninth child from a family of twelve—eight boys and four girls—Graduated Georgia Tech School of Physics. Current close associates—Dr. Sharon Geraldo, daughter of Rear Admiral Rutherford Geraldo. You really should get more friends, David. Shall I go on?"

"No. Who the hell are you?" David asked, annoyed.

"Just call me Didier. I'm from the science investigative arm of Interpol. With the help of the Americans, we've been investigating the organization that runs this facility, and many more like it, for months. They've been implicated in a number of serious offenses—everything from burglary to murder to trafficking in WMD's. They're a real nasty bunch. Your employment here wasn't by happenstance. We needed someone with your qualifications inside. Someone with potential, but not very well known—like a diamond in the ruff, so to speak. Unfortunately, as you can see, our plans didn't go as expected."

"Why wasn't I aware of this?"

"The organization is very secretive and keeps their employees in the dark about what they're working on and why. Most scientists only work on one specific part of a project. That way nobody ever knows the big picture."

"How did I get selected? Does Dr. Geraldo know about this?"

"I'm not sure if your girlfriend is in the loop or how or why you were chosen. You probably impressed someone in your government by something you once did—and of course your association with a high-ranking military official—Admiral Rutherford Geraldo. Obviously, you know the subject matter—and you're easy to control."

"Thanks for nothing," said David.

He felt angry and betrayed. Nothing was more sacred than his private life. He guarded it with an impenetrable shield of silence that kept away those who would use it for nefarious purposes.

A security officer rattled the door handle.

"Time to go, Dr. Woodall," said Didier.

They entered the air duct located in the back of the room. Didier instructed David to close the access cover behind him.

Whatever the immediate destination, it would be a challenging journey. The men crawled and pulled themselves through the narrow conduit. Claustrophobic, David had to stop several times. Didier encouraged him on.

"Think of a happy moment. Something that makes you smile," he said.

David thought of Geri. He missed her—whenever or wherever she was now—he missed her. He wanted to tell her how he really felt about her—how her presence made him fumble his words—the nervous anticipation felt inside at the mere thought of seeing her—how he melted when she touched him . . . and her special smile—a smile the bowels of her soul could not contain.

"Dr. Woodall—Dr. Woodall—you okay?"

"Yeah—sorry, I drifted off there for a minute. Where are we headed anyway?"

"To the elevator shaft," replied Didier.

He removed his PDA from his pocket.

"What's that?"

"Floor plans for the entire facility. I downloaded it several weeks ago when I discovered one of the properties of the Atlantis Ring."

"You used it?"

"Yeah, but I still haven't figured out why it works. I did discover something interesting about the symbols on the ring though. They're similar to pictograms found in a cave in Zhejiang Province, China."

David looked at the ring.

"You think this thing has a Chinese origin?"

"Are you familiar with Chinese philosophy the Yin and Yang?"

"Yin and Yang?"

"The dual concepts of Yin and Yang, which describe two primal opposing but complementary principles or cosmic forces, said to be found in all non-static objects and processes in the universe."

"Sorry, doesn't ring a bell."

"It's the cornerstone of most branches of Chinese philosophy, as well as traditional Chinese medicine."

"Still nothing," said David.

Contrary to his apparent unfamiliarity with the subject matter, because Geri studied Far Eastern values and beliefs, he was very familiar with the early Han dynasty and the Five Agents school of Chinese thought. David wasn't about to give more personal information to Didier freely. The men continued crawling slowly through the air duct.

"The Yin is the dark element. It's passive, dark, negative, downward-seeking, and consuming. The Yang is the bright element. It's active, light, positive, upward-seeking, and producing. The ring, I believe, has the ability to channel the Yang and weakening the Yin cosmic forces. As you witnessed, the residual effects are even transferable to anyone that's exposed to the hand of the wearer," explained Didier.

"Really—fascinating," David said sarcastically.

He still didn't trust Didier.

They came to a junction in the conduit. Didier looked at the facility's schematics on his PDA.

"This way," said Didier.

He noticed the change in David's behavior.

"It's standard protocol for field agents to know everything possible about unsuspecting moles, Dr. Woodall. It not only protects me, it also keeps you safe. It's nothing personal."

His words were comforting.

"I'm sorry for being so abrupt earlier. Dr. Geraldo, a group of scientists and a team of soldiers were exploring an underwater structure off the coast of Indonesia when they suddenly disappeared and I'm a little shaken up about it."

"What were they doing there?"

"They were trying to recover an artifact identical to the one located in the lab."

"The Kronotus Sphere?"

"You're familiar with it?"

"The commission, the organization that runs this facility and many others just like it, killed a paleontologist along with an airplane full of people just to get their hands on it," said Didier.

"Well, I was conducting experiments, subjecting it to certain types of cosmic radiation at different levels, when I noticed it emitting strange subatomic particles. I thought the unidentifiable radiation might be gravitons or tachyons. It wasn't until Admiral Geraldo told me that Geri had gone missing did I realize what probably happened."

"Gravitons—so you believed the sphere is a time displacement device."

"Yes. Somehow, the technology when activated is able to distort space-time. It confused me at first because the particles had peculiar characteristics."

"What characteristics?" Didier asked.

"They lined up in a certain way—not random like it normally would be. After speaking with Geri's father, I realized what artifact actually did."

"Good heavens—! The device creates a portal, but it's only one way? Let me see if I have this right. Dr. Geraldo and a group of other brave souls decided to go to the bottom of the ocean to retrieve a sphere from a structure that shouldn't be there. Somehow they activate the thing and either was whisked back into time or to the future."

"Probably back in time," said David.

"Why do you think that?" Didier asked.

"The particles lined up negative to positive, creating octahedrons. They then form matrixes that seem to fluctuate," David replied.

"Therefore, the movement of the particles is not multidirectional, which means matter can only flow one way when the object is initialized. It also means that a receiver is necessary to complete and terminate the process. So, you thought by activating the artifact it would create a door for them to step through . . . back into our time."

"That was the general idea," said David. "Dr. Jamison was overwhelmed by it."

"Where is he? Is he dead?" asked Didier.

"The question is when . . . not where. He's someplace in the past," answered David.

"They chose well when they selected you for this operation, Dr. Woodall. Obviously, you know do your stuff; you just need to trust in your abilities."

Didier looked at his PDA again.

"We're here."

"Where?"

"The service elevator shaft," said Didier.

He put his PDA in his mouth, freeing up both hands.

"Now if I can just get this panel off."

Didier grabbed both sides and pulled.

"There—piece of cake."

He crawled out on a narrow access ledge.

"Come on, David . . . and be careful. There's not a lot of room."

With Didier's assistance, David slowly exited the air vent behind him.

The shaft was deep, wide, and smelled of refined motor oil. It contained two large hydraulic elevators, each car ferrying supplies and equipment delivered by truck.

"It's a long way down," said David.

Not only was he somewhat claustrophobic, heights also frightened him.

"You're not acrophobic are you?" asked Didier. "You know—afraid of heights?"

"Who me—? Of course not," said David, trying to relax.

He looked down the shaft.

"Yes, I am."

"Don't worry. Just remember what I said earlier. Take deep breaths and think of something pleasant . . . something that brings you joy. You know, Doctor Woodall . . . you're not the first person that's ever been afraid to face your fears. The thing to do is to identify them and ask how they came to be. Then you'll be able to overcome them."

Didier's words touched something inside David, creating an awakening. He took a deep breath.

"Thanks Didier," said David. "I'll be alright".

"Good," said Didier.

He looked at his PDA and pressed several keys.

"What are you doing?" asked David.

"I'm accessing the facility's mainframe so I can override one of the service cars to stop one floor down. Then I'll have it go to the assigned fire service floor, which should be ground level."

"Won't they notice you hacking into the system?"

"Let me worry about that," said Didier. "Here it comes now."

The elevator slowly ascended along the jack and traveling cables. Complaining bitterly, the car moaned and shuddered loudly. A cloud of smoke rose from beneath.

David stared at Didier.

"What? The old service elevators were the best option I could come up with on such short notice. When the car arrives we'll have to jump on top and enter from the roof if it's clear," said Didier. "Be careful touching the cables . . . they can be dangerous if there's any fraying."

The elevator came to rest five feet below where the men stood.

"I'll go first," said Didier.

He placed the PDA in his jacket, then leaned over the edge of the narrow platform and jumped, grabbing a cable. Positioning the towline between his legs, Didier lowered himself onto the car.

"Okay, now your turn," he said.

David looked down. The smell of smoke and motor oil made him hesitant.

"You sure this thing is safe?" asked David.

"Would you rather take your chances with the commission?" asked Didier.

David removed his jacket and wrapped it around his hands.

"I don't think that's a good— . . ."

David jumped, grabbed a tether and slid down.

"Idea." said Didier.

He looked at David in surprise.

"Good Job. Now we're going to ride on top all the way up. That way if someone looks inside, they won't find anybody and they'll just think the elevator is malfunctioning. As soon as it's clear, we enter the car and open the door. Got it?"

"Got it," said David.

Didier removed the PDA and sent the *"assigned fire service floor"* command. The elevator lurched upward, then came to a stop.

"Uh oh," said Didier.

He re-entered the command. The car groaned and lurched again, slowly crawling toward the surface.

"There—that did it," said Didier proudly.

#

In the Operations Center, Dr. Willoughby continued to coordinate the search for the fraudulent employee. He radioed Colonel Prokopovich.

"Any sign of Dr. Woodall, Colonel?"

"So far the traitor has eluded us. But I will find him—and when I do, he will pay and pay dearly."

"Colonel Prokopovich, need I remind you he is to be taken alive for interrogation? He is in no way to be harmed unless absolutely necessary," said Dr. Willoughby. "I have my people working on activating his monitoring chip. We should have it operational in fifteen minutes. I'll send you his file on your PDA when it's up and running."

An officer stuck his head through Dr. Willoughby's office door.

"We have a fire alarm on one of the old service elevators, sir."

"Colonel, get some of your men over to the southwest corner of the building and check out the old service elevators. We have an alarm showing up from one of the cars."

"Copy that," responded the colonel.

He radioed his men on a secure channel.

"If anyone captures the spy, Woodall, bring him to me first."

#

The elevator neared its destination. David and Didier rode nervously on top of it.

"Still worried about your friend—Dr. Geraldo?" asked Didier.

"She's very important to me," said David.

The elevator crawled on, coming to a stop at the surface.

"What now?" David asked.

"We wait."

"Wait for what?"

"For security to inspect the car. Don't worry, it won't be long before they're here. I activated a sensor on the car. It'll show up in Operations as a fire emergency. You know, David—you must have faith. Can I call you David?"

"Faith? Are you a religious man, Didier?"

"Faith is not just a characteristic of religion. It's also indicative of a successful person, Dr. Woodall. You'll do well to remember that," said Didier.

"Call me David."

It wasn't long before the men heard voices outside the elevator car. Didier held his finger to his lips, signaling David to remain motionless and silent.

"I don't see why we need to check this place out," said an unidentified voice. "These elevators haven't been used for years."

"I agree," replied his cohort. "Who is this guy we are looking for? CIA, KGB, the Mossad Israeli Intelligence? Maybe it's Boris Badenov from the Bullwinkle Show. Hey Rocky, watch me pull a rabbit out of my magic hat. I love that. Moose and squirrel is number one."

The other man laughed. He struggled with the elevator door as his fellow soldier stood guard.

"Give me a hand, Sergei. The door mechanism must be stuck."

"Allow me, comrade," said Sergei.

Placing his automatic weapon against the wall and rolling up his sleeves, he pulled the safety door open, revealing the dimly-lit and musty shaft.

Coughing from the stale air, he leaned over the edge and looked down below.

"See anything?"

"Not yet," said Sergei.

"Give it time. You'll see something soon."

He placed a foot against Sergei's backside and shoved him down the empty shaft. Tumbling head first, the body tangled between the jack and the traveling cables. The soldier removed his flashlight, then shook the restraints, dislodging the corpse. He then picked up Sergei's automatic rifle, tossing it down the empty chute. Emotionless, the assassin moved a few feet right and pushed the call button for the second car.

As the door slowly opened, the soldier drew his side arm.

"Dr. Woodall—I'm here to help you," he announced.

Didier removed the vent from the top of the elevator and eased himself to the car's floor.

"I see you made it," said the soldier.

"Piece of cake," said Didier. "Come on down, David. This gentleman will escort you safely off the premises."

David climbed through the opening. Didier put his hand on his shoulder.

"Remember what I told you, David—have faith and confidence in yourself. You'll get much farther in life if you do."

David removed the ring and handed it to Didier.

"Thank you," said David. "Thank you for everything."

They shook hands, then Didier climbed back atop the elevator. He closed the vent and sent the car back into the abyss.

"Dr. Woodall, my name is Oleksander. I'm a member of the Panther Unit, Ukraine military intelligence. The American government requested assistance with your extraction."

"I hope you have a plan. The place is crawling with security," said David.

"There's a vehicle waiting for you off the grounds, about two and a half kilometers southwest of here. We just have to get you to it. The cameras along that area of the security fence are disabled. When you get there, you'll find an opening large enough for you to crawl through. The driver will take you to the airport and will make sure you get on a flight."

"Okay," said David.

"Here, take this."

Oleksander opened a backpack and handed David a military-style camouflage jacket and pants.

David held the pants against his legs.

"Don't worry, they'll fit. I accessed your file before I took them from the armory and supply depot. You know how to handle a weapon?"

He removed a 9mm Makarov automatic handgun from the pack and checked the clip.

"No, not really," said David, "but I'm a quick study."

"Well, this is simple. Just point and shoot until you run out of ammo. Hopefully, you won't have to use it."

He handed the firearm to David.

"Put it in your waistband behind you, underneath your coat," said Oleksander.

He looked at his watch.

"After you hear an explosion, I want you to run for those trees until you get to the fence. Follow it about ninety meters to the right until you reach the hole. Then follow the stream south until you see a "no dumping" sign. Up the incline, a lady is waiting in a car."

Oleksander looked at his watch again.

"Ready?" Oleksander asked.

David nodded.

He turned the rim of the watch's face left, and then pressed a button on the wristband. An explosion echoed from the far side of the building.

#

At Pterosaur Cave, more Chindesaurus pushed through the enlarged opening caused by the earthquake. The second reptile clamped its jaws around the neck of the fallen soldier. Harris screamed as its serrated teeth grasped his neck, puncturing his windpipe. Despite his injury, TJ, Tank and Dr. Stolte were in full retreat as more animals penetrated the safety of the cavern. With little room to manuver in the narrow corridors, the advantage shifted towards the soliders. They slashed and stabbed repeatedly as the Chindersarus attacked in single file, one after another. Dickerson, Danny Boy and Sergeant Davidson joined the fight. In the chamber the walls glowed, displaying a magnificant aray of hieroglyphs and sparkling lights. Geri ran outside the room.

"Quick, everybody inside. Something is happening."

In the heat of the battle, Tank felt the sphere vibrating. He removed it from his pouch. Mysterious writing illuminated the orb.

"Doc, I think you'll need this," he yelled as he fought off an attacker.

He tossed it to her. She snatched it out of midair with one hand and hurried back into the chamber.

Outside in the corridor, the conflict continued. Sergeant Davidson pulled one of his two remaining grenades from his belt and crammed it between a space outside the entrance. He removed the last stun grenaded and tossed it between the bipeds. The remainder of his ammo went into the lead Chindesaurus. It fell to the floor, temporarily blocking the rest of the reptiles from advancing.

"Get into the chamber," yelled the sergeant.

Muffled by the cavern, the ordinance detonated with a thud, sending debris raining down on beast and man. Geri placed the sphere into a depression atop a pedestal. Three silver prongs extended outward grasped it, locking it into place.

"Everybody get on the platform."

She turned it clockwise, then counter-clockwise. Nothing happened.

"Doc, whatever you're going to do, you'd better do it quick," said Sergeant Davidson, detonating the last grenade remotely.

Positioned at the entrance of the chamber, the debris it caused was their last line of defense.

Fully recovered from the stun grenade, the Chindesaurus scratched and clawed at the rocks outside the entrance. Geri looked around the chamber. She glanced at the eight larger stones and the four smaller ones.

"Eight and four, eight and four equals twelve. Too easy—think, think. Eight, eight— . . ."

"Hurry up, Doc. That's not going to hold them off for long," said the sergeant.

"It's a time displacement device, so think in terms of time—seven days in a week, eight days represents—represents—beyond seven days—beyond time. Good, good—four, four—four seasons—four—four—time and three-dimensional space together—space time. I think I've got it."

She glanced surreptitiously at her device, then rotated the orb eight times right and four times left. As the reptiles broke through, an intense radiance consumed the commandos and scientists. It startled the animals briefly, causing them to hesitate. The alpha attacked. It leaped through the air shrieking, mouth agape and claws ready. Professor Rosenbaum screamed as the illumination and the group disappeared.

The soldiers held their combat knives to the hand-to-hand position as the darkness surrounding the group slowly lifted.

#

The temperature outside the Spirit Cave had plummeted to thirty-nine degrees below zero. Kanut and his grandfather, an old shaman, sat next to a small fire to keep warm. Resin-covered flowers, collected hundreds of miles away, burned in carved mammoth bones. Its fragrance filled the chamber, tempting spirits to partake in a blending between the dead and the undead. With eyes closed, the shaman beat rhythmically on a caribou skin-covered drum and chanted an ancient Inuit mantra.

"Kadzait niovgroyok angelrauwok pianikpok ingelrayok. Takungartut tireksorpok anersarpok satuiyok piungineruti-wok..."

Kanut shielded his eyes as a brilliant luminance overran the dimly-lit chamber. It quickly vanished. Cautiously, Sergeant Davidson stepped off the platform.

"Where are we? What is this place?" he asked Kanut.

"The place of my ancestors. We have traveled far to meet you. Are you spirits?"

"No. We're not spirits."

Kanut's grandfather continued to chant.

"What is he doing?" Sergeant Davidson asked.

"He sings of wandering wolves traveling far away. The spirit lights returned them home safely. Their journey over, the caribou, the seal and the fish in the sea will multiply abundantly."

"It's Inuit," said Geri. "We're probably somewhere around northern Canada."

"She's right, Sergeant," said Tank. "GPS says about fifty miles from the Artic circle."

"Good. Looks like we made it. Danny Boy, see if you can raise anybody on SatCom."

"Black jackal to foxhole, over. Black jackal to foxhole, over."

The rest of the team stepped from the platform.

"Dr. Geraldo, can I speak to you for a minute—privately?"

"Sure, Seargeant Davidson. What's up?"

He pulled her to the side.

"Look Doc, if there's anything I understand it is the need to protect classified information. But if we ever work together again and you put civilians or my men in danger by not disclosing critical information, I'll make sure you're the one left behind next time."

"What do you mean? What information?"

"For one, you knew exactly how that orb thing worked. I saw you when you accessed the information from your device. I'll let you in on a little known fact to people like us, Doc. Life isn't always black or white—when you throw people into the mix, it's mostly grey. And when there's people involved, that's where your prioity should be. Not the mission."

Geri stood there speechless. She understood exactly what the sergeant was saying. In her zeal to succeed, she had compromised her values. She felt alone.

The shaman stood up.

"Welcome, my lost friends," he said.

He removed a thin necklace from around his neck and pressed it into the palm of Sergeant Davidson's hand.

"Thank you," said the sergeant.

He opened his hand and saw Harris' dog tags—his soldier that died over two hundred million years ago.

#

Attempting to reach his rendezvous point, David plodded through thick brush and trees.

After hearing dogs barking off in the distance, he progressed more rapidly. Surprisingly, he felt at peace, his demons silent. He hadn't experienced such clarity since he could remember. He focused on the future—his future. With a newfound confidence, his unrealized dreams were finally real and achievable. As he reached the vehicle, his cell phone rang.

"Hello, this is Dr. Woodall."

"David, this is Admiral Geraldo. I just got a call from Geri."

"Is she alright? Where is she?" David asked.

"She's fine, but there were several casualties. They're somewhere in the Artic. A rescue team out of Eielson Air Force Base is headed there now."

"Thank God it worked," said David, relieved.

"What worked? Did you have anything to do with them showing up thousands of miles away?"

"I'll explain later, Admiral. Will they be debriefed in Fairbanks?"

"Yeah, for a couple of days at least . . . I'll meet you there and David . . . thank you. I won't forget what you've done to bring my baby home safely," said Admiral Geraldo, his voice trembling.

"You're welcome, sir. I'll be in Alaska by tomorrow."

He closed his cell phone. That moment, he understood something about himself he'd never realized. He'd had the power to overcome his demons all along. They led him to believe that mediocrity was enough because it's safe. However, mediocrity destroys self-confidence and breeds habit . . . and habit sings a siren's song.

As his driver drove over the bridge leading to Zurich International Airport, David motioned for her to stop. He turned to her and smiled.

"Today you begin anew, for you, and only you, are the master of your abilities."

Confused, the Swiss woman glanced at David and drove on.

The Atlantis Ring had left him with one final and lasting gift . . . clarity of purpose.

THE END

Printed in the United States
149932LV00007BA/206/P